Every Story Is A Love Story

For Travis & Joyce,
So nice to meet you!
all the best,
John

Every Story Is A Love Story

John Moncure Wetterau

Fox Print Books

Creative Commons
559 Nathan Abbott Way
Stanford, California 94305, USA.

Published by: Fox Print Books
45 Pleasant Ave
Peaks Island, ME 04108
foxprintbooks@gmail.com

Cover painting: *hummingbirds* by Paul Brahms, used with his permission.

This is a work of fiction. Names, characters, places and incidents either are the product of the author's imagination or are used fictitiously, and any resemblance to any actual persons, living or dead, events, or locales is entirely coincidental.

Acknowledgements:

Thanks to Larry Dake, Christopher Evers, Bruce Gordon, Majo Keleshian, Jane Lowenstein, Sylvester Pollet, and Nancy Wallace for valuable suggestions and invaluable support. Gino's poem, *Aesthetic*, is by Sylvester Pollet and is used with his permission. Thanks, also, to Paul Brahms for the cover painting. More of his work can be seen at: www.paulbrahms.com.

Contents

For Rosy

Thy love is better than high birth to me,
Richer than wealth, prouder than garment's cost,
Of more delight than hawks or horses be;

Sonnet XCI
WILLIAM SHAKESPEARE

Chapter 1

A red MG came racketing around the corner. It passed, stopped, and reversed, one front fender swinging freely.

"Where you going?" The driver had wild eyes and a two day growth.

"Woodstock."

"Get in, get in." Patrick lowered himself into the small seat, holding his AWOL bag on his lap. "Whisky in the JAR," the driver sang to himself shifting through gears. "Musharingum-googee . . . WAK for the Daddy-O . . . " He turned and shouted over the engine, "Where you coming from?"

"Wiesbaden."

"Germany?"

"Yes," Patrick shouted back.

"WAK for the Daddy-O . . . Good beer, the Krauts." They flew off bumps and jolted around curves for five or six miles. Conversation was impossible. They passed a golf course, rolling and open before a dark wall of mountain, then climbed a hill by three gas stations. "Woodstock!" the driver shouted, stopping at a narrow triangular green.

"Thanks for the ride."

The sound of the MG diminished in the distance as Patrick

looked around at trees, a neatly painted white church, and a row of stores. He walked in the direction that the MG had gone until he reached a field about a mile from the green. He turned back and stopped at a house that had a large porch and a sign announcing "ROOMS."

An older woman answered his ring. Her hair was white, elaborately piled above her head.

"I'd like to rent a room—if you have any vacancies."

"Hmmph." She was shorter than Patrick but seemed to be looking down at him. "This is a quiet house."

"Yes, ma'am."

"No smoking."

"Yes, ma'am."

She opened the door and showed him a corner room with a matching bed and bureau and a small rocking chair. "Bathroom down the hall." He paid for a week and signed the guest register. "O'Shaunessy?"

"Yes."

She handed him two keys. "I lock the front door after dark." Patrick nodded and retreated to the room. He unpacked his clothes and a paperback copy of The Origin of Species which he placed on the bedside table. He lay on the bed a few minutes adjusting to his new home, then left, closing the door silently behind him.

In town, he decided to try the Cafe Espresso. He walked down wide stone steps, crossed a patio, and entered an open door. Two people at the end of a small bar leaned towards each other, laughing and talking in lowered tones. At the other end of the room, a young man was practicing on an upright piano.

Patrick sat at a window table and waited until a tall woman emerged from the kitchen. She wore bead necklaces, a tight gray jersey, and a wrap around red and orange Indian print skirt. A thick blonde braid hung to her waist. Patrick ordered rice and vegetables and watched her hips move to a gentle repeating melody from the piano. The player varied the tempo and the emphasis, working further into the piece, exploring its edges without losing its rhythmic heart.

A man in his thirties with a round face and curly hair came in and sat at the next table. He placed black and white stones on a Go board, studying each move.

"That is Go, isn't it? I've read about it," Patrick offered.

"Go is an ancient Japanese game," the player said without looking up. "It requires intelligence and concentration."

"That leaves me out," Patrick said. The couple at the bar walked out. As the woman passed through the door, she looked back at Patrick and smiled. Her eyes were gray, her shoulders half-turned, her weight evenly balanced. She was about 21, his age. He smiled back, surprised.

Women didn't usually pay attention to Patrick. He was compact, medium sized. He had reddish-brown hair and a square face with high cheekbones and traces of freckles. His blue eyes were set deeply behind thick eyebrows. He had been called "cute" a couple of times. Mostly he got sympathetic smiles as women pushed past him, going for the tall, dark, and handsomes, or the ones with money, or the major losers. It was a mystery to him how people got coupled up.

"My name is Eve," the waitress said in a luxurious voice as she bent forward with his plate. She had goddess breasts and smelled of patchouli.

"I'm Patrick," he said and choked. "King of repartee," he added, regaining his voice. She smiled as if she had known him deeply in another life, and then she swayed away into the kitchen. The Go player remained immersed in study, an air of relief emanating from his face. Perhaps he was recovering from the attentions of dark beauties with trust funds. Don't be jealous, Patrick told himself. When the gods want a good laugh, they give you what you want. "Try me," another voice in him said. "Long dark hair."

He ate dinner and began to confront the next problem. He had a few travelers checks in reserve, but he'd always found work before he had to cash them. He had paid for his own flight back to Wiesbaden.

"Come on, Pat, let me pay," his father offered.

"Nope."

"You're a hard case, Patrick."

It had been a good visit, but Patrick was ready to go after a week. "I thought I'd try Woodstock, New York," he told his father. "You used to talk about it."

"My old stomping grounds," his father said. "I have a friend there, Heidi Merrill. Haven't heard from her since her husband died. She has a son. Look her up for me, Pat—give her my best."

"Will do."

Patrick checked around the cafe for a pay phone, wondering whether there was a listing for his father's friend. No phone. On his way out of the cafe, he changed his mind and ordered a beer at the bar. The room was filling. A Van Morrison album had replaced the piano player. Attractive women crowded around guys who wore hammer hooks and Stanley tapes like jewelry on their belts, totems of a better way.

"Feels good to stand up," he said to the guy next to him. "This is a happening place."

"You just get here?"

"Yep. Any work around?"

"What kind of work?"

"Wash dishes, construction, paint houses . . . "

"Hey Parker, you need anybody?" A heavyset fellow came over. He had a pleasant ironic expression.

"For what?" There were white paint stains on his button-down blue shirt.

"Says he's looking for work."

"Patrick O'Shaunessy." Patrick extended his hand.

"Parker Ives." He looked Patrick over as they shook hands. "Ladders, Patrick. Wasps," he said.

"No problem."

"Good. Meet me in the News Shop at 8; we'll see how it goes."

"Tomorrow?" Patrick asked.

"And tomorrow and—yes." Parker drained the glass of beer he was holding. "Tomorrow." He put his glass on the bar and left.

"Parker's all right. My name is Claude, by the way."

"Aieee, Claude! A thin blonde with green eye shadow and exaggerated cherry red lipstick put her arms around his neck.

"Excuse me, Patrick."

Two young women entered and came over to the bar. One of them bent over, removed a sandal, and shook it. She had waist length dark brown hair and was wearing Levi's and a blue chambray shirt. She had long legs and long arms that made interesting angles out from the crouching curve of her hips. "There," she said, straightening. The top three buttons of her shirt were undone. Sensitive, Patrick thought. Her eyes were unusually clear, light hazel with flecks of gray and green. Her blonde friend was shorter, narrow waisted, and well built. The blonde caught him looking. Patrick, reddening, thought he saw a flash of understanding. She was a thinker, might even have read a book lately.

In Patrick's second year at Florida State, a biology professor named Ted Williams had turned him on to science. Patrick was an Army brat; he had lived in Florida, the Philippines, Panama, and Germany. He spoke passable Spanish and German. His parents were readers. Patrick had been around books all his life and felt as though he were ahead of the other students. Once he found a direction—that he wanted to learn more about science— he decided to go right at it. He didn't have to be a university student to read the books. It would be cheaper, and, besides, people were on the move. Work was easy to come by.

His father, raised in the depression and caught up in World War II, had stayed in the army. "Never underestimate the importance of a good billet," he had told Patrick more than once, an edict laid on him by Sergeant Donald, a mythic presence from the days before Officer Candidate School. Patrick's father never tired of quoting Sergeant Donald as they moved from base to base.

His parents were patient and generally good humored about military life. They escaped into books. When Patrick announced that he was dropping out, his father seemed to think it was fine. "Don't burn any bridges, Pat. You can go back to school later, if you want. Or come work with me." His father was about to retire from the Army and was planning to settle in Florida and work for himself as a handyman. When his father wasn't reading, he enjoyed fixing things; he looked forward to becoming a sort of anti-hero—Major O'Shaunessy to the rescue, the tools, the truck, the little boxes of washers and screws and finishing nails, the retirement checks punctually in the mail.

Patrick's mother fussed about Patrick's eating habits, but she wasn't really worried. Patrick's sister, Molly, had earned a commercial pilot's license before she settled down in Atlanta to teach English, married to a hard working good old boy. Patrick, his mother felt, would find his own way if he ate right and got enough sleep. Both parents suggested books for his reading list.

Patrick was well along in the list. When he finished books, he mailed them to Molly for safekeeping. Building the library, he would tell himself as he doled out postage money. Another few days and he would send the Darwin.

He was still looking at the blonde. She smiled slightly, and he said, "I'm Patrick."

"Amber," she said. "This is my friend, Willow." Patrick nodded at them both and moved a step closer.

"I like this place," he said.

"First time in the Depresso?"

Patrick laughed. "Is that what you call it?"

"That's what everybody calls it," Amber said. "How long have you been in town?"

"About four hours."

Amber touched Willow's arm. "We're old timers."

"We've been here a month," Willow said in a low voice. There was a brief drop in the noise level as the piano player crossed the room with quick steps and went out the door. "There he goes," Amber said.

"Who's he?" asked Patrick.

"Dylan. He's Willow's hero."

"Dylan?"

"Bob Dylan," Willow said.

"No shit," Patrick said.

"He's one of the reasons we're in this whistle stop," Amber said. "Willow heard he was here."

"And Joan Baez and Van Morrison," Willow said.

Patrick snorted. "Where's Beethoven?"

"He's watching, maybe," Willow said.

"My man," Patrick said. "He sure rattled his cage." Willow flushed.

"Van Morrison rattles my cage," Amber said, and Patrick forgot about Beethoven.

"So, what do you do?" he asked her.

"I go to Stanford. We both do."

"I went to Florida State for a while. What are you studying?"

"Pre-med, I guess. My father's a doc."

"I'm reading a lot of science," Patrick said. "Just finishing Darwin."

"Yeah, Darwin," Amber said. "I was in the Galapagos Islands once."

"What! What were they like?"

"Kind of rocky. Foggy in the mornings when I was there. Nothing to do."

Patrick was impressed. "Darwin was good. He kept track. He thought about what he was seeing . . . those finch."

"Yeah," Amber said. She looked around the room. "The usual suspects," she said to Willow. "Long-tailed carpenters," she added for Patrick. It had been a full day. Things were happening too fast; Patrick wanted to slow down.

"Look," he said, "nice to meet you. I'll see you around. I've got a job—start tomorrow."

"Bye, Patrick," Amber said. Willow lifted one hand.

"Amber!" Patrick said to himself, walking back to his room. Frieda had gone to bed with him a couple of times during his last summer in Germany. He'd gotten lucky once at a party in Tallahassee. That was it. No one like Amber. His eyes opened wider as he remembered her. He put his hand on her shoulder, imagining the warm solid body under her white blouse. His mind spun out, and he cleared his throat. He shook his head, got control of himself, and walked faster.

A man playing a blues harp passed him on the other side of Tinker Street. The blues pulsed up into the evening sky, mournful and elaborate, a peacock tail of sound. Feelings stirred for which Patrick had no words. He pumped one fist in the air like a brother and turned aside to the rooming house.

Chapter 2

He likes you, as usual," Willow said. "And of course you don't care. You are such a bitch, sometimes."

"I am not. I can't help it if he likes me." Amber made a tiny swaggering move with her breasts. "Anyway, he likes you just as much."

"Well, why doesn't he look at me?"

"If you'd wear something besides jeans and work shirts . . ." Amber's pants and short skirts clung to perfect legs. Her blouses were tight. She was averagely good looking. Her face was open and energetic; her hair was chestnut tending to blonde, shoulder length and wavy. Men found themselves looking at her, talking to her, and then—the more they looked, the more they saw. She was faster than they were; she adjusted effortlessly in flight, becoming more serious or more carefree, more cerebral or more passionate under their gaze.

"Men are SO stupid," Willow said.

"Don't you think they're cute sometimes? Even AhnRee with his tan and those big white towels he wraps around his belly at the pool. He's old—God, do you think he's fifty?—but he has those big round dark eyes." AhnRee had picked up Amber the second day they were in town.

"When I see someone so special, I know! I must paint you. My name is AhnRee," he had said with great dignity.

"AhnRee?" Willow asked.

"As in Matisse," he said. "It is an honor, such a name. A curse . . . But never mind." He smiled gallantly. Gigi, Willow said to herself. No one should copy Maurice Chevalier. They get the eyes and the teeth, but they don't have the engine. No fire engine inside the doors.

"No fire engine," she said to Amber. "Huh?" AhnRee had said something to Amber and Amber was asking why they shouldn't try living in his studio.

"You will find it most private," AhnRee said. "It is some distance from the main house. In return, a bit of modeling, say, once a week? Say you will," he pleaded.

"Only if it is all right with Willow," Amber said, kicking Willow in the ankle.

"Ah, Willow," AhnRee said, wrenching his eyes from Amber who was becoming ever more elusive, more of a muse.

"Where is this place?" Willow asked.

"A short drive up the mountain. An easy ride on a bicycle. In fact, I have several bicycles—if you don't mind the old fashioned kind with baskets on the handlebars."

"And what do I have to do?" Amber kicked her again.

AhnRee considered. "You may mow the lawn around the studio. And, if you wish, attend a little to the flowers."

Willow had given in, and it had been fine. AhnRee had left them alone. And Amber seemed to enjoy modeling. "It's not so bad, being admired," she told Willow.

"Well," Willow said, coming back to the present, "you knocked Patrick out with that bit about foggy mornings on the Galapagos Islands."

"Can I help it if my father is a Darwin freak? He practically made me go with him."

"Christ," Willow said.

"He likes you; I'm telling you," Amber said.

"Gee, maybe he'll let me hold his hand someday, comfort his broken heart." She smiled to soften the edge in her tone, and they pedaled toward home in the early evening light.

Willow liked Patrick. He thought for himself. And his eyes were cute, a penetrating blue that changed from hard to soft. He was the right height and looked strong underneath that funny European work shirt. Her imagination slowed at his belt. She had shared sleeping bags with Aaron at a sing-out, but it had been dark. It had been pleasant enough, I mean, O.K., she wrote in her journal, but men's bodies were basically terra incognita. What she knew of sex was a fuzzy blend of Michelangelo and the diaries of Anais Nin. There were plenty of men around—it wasn't that—it was just that none of them turned her on. She tired of their talk and endless competition. She'd rather listen to the Beethoven quartets. That was another thing about Patrick. What did he say? "Rattled his cage," that was it. Exactly. Her perfect brother, David, said he liked Beethoven; David always said what he was supposed to. But he never listened to Beethoven. He liked the Beatles, for God's sake. I mean, yes, they wrote some catchy melodies, but really. They were a long way from Dylan, let alone Beethoven.

Willow's indignation carried her to the top of the last hill before AhnRee's driveway. She got off her bike and waited for Amber. They walked up the bumpy dirt road, one on each side of the grass strip in the middle. As they passed the main house, they got on their bikes and pedaled to the studio along the edge of a small steep hay field rich in clover and wildflowers, surrounded by trees. The studio was made of dark weathered wood. It had a deep glow to Willow, perhaps because it was the first time she had lived anywhere other than home or the university.

She slept on a screened porch that looked into the woods

behind the house. Amber had the bedroom. The central room had a cathedral ceiling and a skylight that faced north. It was furnished with an old couch, a coffee table, and two armchairs drawn up by a stone fireplace. They ate at a large table in the kitchen, the room through which one entered the house.

AhnRee explained to Amber that skylights faced north so that the light for painting would be more even, the changes more gradual. Painters had been settling in Woodstock for generations. There were many such houses—hard to keep warm in the winter, but, AhnRee pointed out with a shrug, "If one is in San Miguel d'Allende . . . "

"Mexico, right?" Willow asked Amber.

"Right. I guess he goes there every winter." Amber had spent her time meeting people and going to parties. She already had one guy chasing her, showing up unannounced and hanging around. Willow usually excused herself and read on her bed. An outside door led to the porch; the door was solid and blocked most of the noise from inside the house. When she wasn't reading, she took walks and rode her bike into town for groceries. She was learning to cook. You would have killed a robin if you hit it with her first loaf of seven grain bread, but she was getting the hang of it. She had developed a wicked lasagna. Mornings after, the lasagna pan was as empty as the Chianti bottle or bottles.

On this particular evening, she threw a salad together—avocado, feta cheese, a few scallions, red leaf lettuce, lemon juice, and a yummy Portuguese olive oil that Ann-in-the-deli had recommended. Ann was middle aged with a red face and a bad leg. She sat behind the cash register, talking loudly with customers, denouncing the government and its stupid war. She liked young people and extended credit when they were short of money. She had a metal box with 3X5 cards in it, alphabetized by name. Willow watched her accept payments and cross out numbers at the bottom of little columns while customers waited proudly with bags containing six-packs, cigarettes, potato chips, and quarts of milk. If someone was charging, he (usually a he) would mumble thanks and pick his way out guiltily while Ann added another number to his column.

"I've got to get a job soon," Willow said, taking another bite of salad.

"What for?" Amber's father made a deposit every month to her account. While you're in school, he told her.

"I want to. I mean, I don't want to keep living on your money."

"It's not my money. I didn't earn it."

"Yeah, but . . . " They had taken a bus to Sacramento and caught a train east, the day after finals. The idea swept them off their feet. They were just now, a month later, realizing that they were actually somewhere else. After a day of walking around the Village in New York, they took a bus to Woodstock. They got out in front of the News Shop, and here they were. Their parents weren't thrilled, but Amber convinced her father on the phone that she was having a good time and was in control of herself. Willow resorted to a stream of postcards—maple trees in October, scenes of the Ashokan Reservoir, and one of the tiny Old Catholic Church peeping out of the trees. "Father Francis built it himself with the help of his boys, I mean, acolytes," she wrote. "A kindly old fraud who presides over his two acres with tottering good humor, dispensing advice and tea to wanderers. Amber and I went to a wedding there last week. Lots of flowers. Lousy cake. It's halfway up a mountain called, `Overlook.' Love, Willow."

"What would you do?" Amber asked.

"I don't know. I don't think I'm waitress material. I mean, God, I wish I were. I like food, but I'm too dreamy. I mean, I want to do something well."

"You don't want to work at night, anyway," Amber said.

"No." When it got dark, Willow would just as soon go to bed with a book. She was an early riser.

"Go with the flow," Amber said. "Something will turn up."

"I guess." Willow collected the dishes, washed them, and went out to the porch, to her comfortable bed, a warm safe cave. She undressed and snuggled into her pillows. Darwin, she thought. She imagined Patrick aboard H.M.S. Beagle. "Your muffin, Sir." She presented him with a gorgeous cinnamon apple muffin on a tin plate. "Aye, aye," someone said as she fell asleep.

In the morning, she went for a walk, gathered wildflowers for the kitchen table, and mixed a batch of bread, placing it to rise in the sun, covered with a dishcloth. She made coffee and ate a bagel. Amber appeared, yawning and rubbing her eyes. She poured herself a cup of coffee, and they discussed the day's possibilities. Art wanted Amber to help him prepare a barnwarming party; he had just bought a barn that he planned to make into a house. Willow was invited. Art was considerate and rather handsome, Willow conceded. But she thought she'd stay home. "How are you going to meet people that way?" Amber asked.

"I'm already meeting people," she said. "I'm bored with people."

Amber shook her head. "Do you think I ought to let my hair get longer? This coffee is so good."

"Long hair is a pain," Willow said dismissively, although she was proud of hers and brushed it thoroughly every day. "With your body, who needs distraction?"

"I don't know. I look so—conventional." This was dangerous territory. Amber was, in fact, conventional. She was a little wild, maybe, but she was on the pill and she didn't get attached for long; she kept her options open. Her grades were surprisingly good. Willow's own record at Stanford was ordinary. The courses were all so canned, pre-digested, just right for her perfect brother who was a year behind her and practically in law school already. Willow did the minimum, but she wasn't into it. There had to be more to life than the accepted opinion about George Eliot. Christ, you were lucky if you got to read James Joyce, never mind Henry Miller. Willow adored Henry Miller.

"All right, I am conventional," Amber said, breaking into Willow's reverie. "And I'm going to have a damned good time while I'm at it." Willow poured the last of the coffee into their cups. Amber wasn't really awake, Willow knew. At ten or eleven, her eyes would open the rest of the way, slightly startled, slightly pleased to have survived the transition. Amber's eyes were a dark Mediterranean brown. If I were gay, Willow thought, I could go for Amber. She's so fierce underneath that easy chameleon surface; she knows what she wants, and she gets it. Amber stretched and went back into her room, emerging when Art honked the horn in his pickup. Willow waved at Art and watched Amber skip into the truck, elaborately casual, a barnwarmer's dream. Willow punched down the bread and left it to rise again. Amber would get fucked tonight, she thought. Or not. But she'd have the choice.

Willow washed the few dishes and dried them as she tried to think about sex. It was becoming a more persistent question or urge or need, these days. She wandered out to the porch, kicked off her sandals, and lay on the bed. She imagined Art standing by the door. He melted down and changed into Patrick. "Oh, to hell with it," she said and took off her pants. She ran her fingers lightly back and forth between her legs while Patrick watched. She drew up her knees. She let them fall open. "What are you looking at?" she teased Patrick in a low voice.

"I'm a romantic," he said earnestly.

"Well, if you're a romantic, why aren't you naked with a

rose in your teeth?" Patrick left, as she continued to play with herself. In a moment, he was back, naked, a long stemmed red rose held carefully between his teeth. He was nicely muscled with a flat stomach. She motioned him closer with one hand. He approached slowly, and she held out her hand for the rose. He gave it to her. "Good, Patrick," she said and struck him lightly across the stomach. Thorns left three tiny drops of blood. He gasped and drew in his stomach. His eyes opened wider and softened. "What do you want?" she asked.

"To please you." She looked at the rose, weighed it in her hand to get the feel of it, and looked back at Patrick. He did not run away. He was willing to suffer for her. His mouth was slightly open and he had a large erection. She indicated the end of the bed with the rose and slid down, pulling a pillow with her for her head. Patrick moved around in front of her. She pointed at the flagstones of the porch floor.

"So, please me." He got on his knees and she placed her heels on his back. Willow's knees were slowly opening and closing as she rubbed harder. Her long slim back arched. Patrick. "Ahhh," she cried softly. "Ahhhhhhh, ahhhh, ahhh." Her feet slid out and her legs collapsed on the bed. She was warm and wet and out of breath. She opened her eyes. The air was bright, almost vivid. Patrick had disappeared. She would reward him another time. Laundry, she thought cheerfully.

A crow called twice. She rolled over on her side and watched a squirrel jump onto the trunk of a maple and wait, tail curled, listening. "Squirrelie," she said. "Yes." She sat up, swinging her feet down to the cool flagstones. "Yes," she said. "Shower." Squirrelie ran up the tree out of view.

Willow made a pile of clothes on the cotton coverlet and took the bundle to the washing machine in a corner of the kitchen. She pulled off her T-shirt and walked into the bathroom where she regarded herself in the mirror before getting into the shower.

Her breasts were too small, she thought as hot water ran deliciously down her back; but they were pretty. Her long waist and long legs gave her body a flowing athletic line. I do have an adequate ass, she said to herself, soaping it. She was continually unsure as to whether she should throw it around or wait until The Right One discovered it for himself.

"You are so beautiful," The Right One said, unable to lift his eyes. She swayed modestly.

"I have these three tasks," she said and burst out laughing in the shower. The bread, God. She washed her hair and went on with the day.

Amber returned mid-afternoon and was unable to convince her to go to the party. Shortly after Amber left, Willow considered the house (clean), her hair (brushed), and the rest of the day (free). She put a paperback copy of *Big Sur and the Oranges of Hieronymus Bosch* in her bag and rode out past Ah-nRee's. He was drinking something by the pool, accompanied by a placid looking blonde in her forties. Willow waved and then bumped down to the blacktop road where she picked up speed and breezed downhill into town, her hair fluttering nicely behind her.

She was early enough to get a table on the patio in front of the Depresso. She ordered a cup of coffee and read her book, looking up now and then to watch the regulars gather and the tourists walk uncomfortably back and forth. Her porch, the clean house, and the baked bread were satisfyingly present.

"What are you reading?" God! Patrick was standing a few feet away. She held the book so that he could read the cover. "I've come for my reward," he said. She dropped the book. "A cold one after a day of scraping paint," he continued, reaching down and handing her the book. "Henry Miller—I heard he was good."

"Yes," Willow said, recovering. "Well, don't let me keep

you from your reward; you deserve it."

"Right," Patrick said uncertainly. "Willow, right?" She nodded. "Where's Amber?"

"She's at a barnwarming party breaking hearts." This was definitely disloyal.

"Aha," Patrick said, "talk to you later." Willow smiled and went back to her book. I hate him, she thought. Amber, too. She drank the rest of her coffee. Time to leave. But she couldn't bring herself to get on her bike and pedal home.

She went inside and ordered a beer at the bar. Patrick was in deep conversation with a rugged good looking regular named Wendell. They seemed to be talking about chisels. Jesus. Bob Dylan was sitting with Bernard and Marylou, the owners, at a round table near the kitchen door. They were laughing loudly. Bernard has a handsome mustache, Willow thought. Dylan looked like he was winding up for an intense night. He was SO intuitive; he always caught her looking and usually ignored her. Once, he gave her a quick little shake of his head—it's a fucked up world, we gotta do something, he seemed to be saying. He was on the edge of control, major chutzpah.

Willow couldn't get her father to understand Dylan. Her father was a Brahms expert; how could he? "A generational difference," he suggested. Willow had snorted, angry with him for evading the argument. "Far be it from me to suggest that he is a nihilist, simultaneously outdated and immature . . . not to mention noisy," her father continued. Well, at least he wasn't treating her like a child.

"He is writing American masterpieces," she said.

"God help us." Her father was grinning, and they left it at that.

Claude came in and gave her his big smile and automatic wink. He was handsome and could get away with anything, she thought. Damn him. But she had to admit that she liked him.

I mean, he liked himself; everyone in the place liked him; how could she not? Claude began talking to Sue, a painter who was usually with a sad charmer named Jim. As she was thinking about Jim, he came through the door. He and Sue exchanged smiles and private greetings, but they did not hug. He seemed more interested in getting a drink as fast as he could. Problems, Willow thought.

Wendell introduced Patrick to a guy named Joe. The three sat at a table and began talking about the war. Patrick waved Willow over. "You know Willow?" he asked the others.

"Seen you around," Wendell said. Joe nodded. He had looked Willow over on previous occasions in the Depresso. He was tall and alert, in his mid-twenties; he had dark hair, blue eyes, and a mustache. They had never spoken, but Willow had the feeling that he knew more about her than she did about him.

"What do you think about Vietnam?" Patrick asked Willow as she sat down. They waited while she considered.

"I think we ought to take care of our own problems before we start telling other people what to do. And we should be dropping food and medicine, not bombs; I mean, we're killing people." Joe held up his glass in agreement.

"The fucking government is bullshitting us," Wendell said.

"My father's in the Army," Patrick said. "He says we can't win in Asia; look what happened to the French."

"They're bullshitting us," Joe agreed. "But, they believe some of the bullshit—that crap about communism; they want to keep winning the World War. They aren't too bright."

"That's for sure," Patrick said. "My father's getting out."

"The last year I was in," Joe said, "we lost our clerk. The Major made me the clerk because I was the only one who knew how to type. We had this guy, Captain Sampson, who went by the book. He used to send guys back to the barracks if their socks weren't right. He was O.K., really; he thought it was what he was supposed to do—keep the troops sharp, good for morale, and so on. He didn't know any better." Joe took a swallow of beer.

"One day I got an emergency message addressed to Captain Sampson. Why hadn't he reported for his plagu shot? They left off the `e' in plague. I knew right away what had happened. His Nam orders had gotten lost somewhere. I took the message over to him and watched him turn pale. Bye, bye, Sammy, I said to myself. They were just grabbing people for Nam when I got out."

"I had a college deferment for a while," Patrick said. "I hope I don't get drafted. I'd probably leave the country."

"Canada?" Wendell asked.

"South America or Europe," Patrick said.

"I'd never go," Wendell said. "I wouldn't do their dirty work, the assholes."

"They don't want old men, anyway," Joe said.

"I may be old," Wendell said, "but I can put you on your ass, Joe Burke."

"So could Willow," Joe said, grinning.

"It's a female thing," Willow said to Wendell who might or might not be accepting this.

"Female thing," he said looking at her breasts. This was comfortable territory. "Ha, ha. There's male things, and there's female things."

Joe held up his glass. "Right on, Wendell."

Willow finished her beer and left. They were a pretty decent bunch, she thought as she pedaled home. They treated her like one of the guys, almost. She was getting used to conversations full of fuck this and fuck that. It was a relief after the cautious academic world of her parents. When she arrived home, she was flushed from the ride. Amber was still out. She made a sandwich and went to bed with Henry Miller who was dependably self-involved, hip, sexy, and good humored.

Chapter 3

The next morning, in the News Shop, Parker Ives introduced Patrick to Wilson. "Willy, you and Patrick get started on the Van Slyke house." He rubbed his forehead. "She's intense about her roses; better cover them. The lilacs, too. I'll be around later with more primer."

"Ya, Boss. Let's go, Patrick." Wilson was short and muscular, balding, with a thick black mustache and a glass eye. He drove at top speed up the mountain, stopping several miles from town in the driveway of a white Colonial. Purple lilacs leaned out from each side of the front door; rose bushes extended to the ends of the house. They covered the roses with drop cloths and tied a tarpaulin around each lilac. A woman wearing linen slacks and a cafe-au-lait blouse appeared at the corner of the house. Her hair was blonde, short, and well cut.

"Good morning. Is Parker here?"

"He will be, later," Wilson said. She nodded and drove away in a station wagon, tires crunching on gravel.

They worked on ladders, scraping a section and then priming it. "Willy—is every woman in Woodstock good looking?" Patrick asked.

"Depends how long you look," Wilson said. Parker drove in,

and Wilson jumped from the fourth rung of his ladder. "Break time." They walked over to Parker's aging blue Mercedes.

"How you doing, Patrick?"

"He's having a little trouble with the pace," Willy said sitting down, placing his coffee on the grass.

"Up yours," said Patrick.

"But for what you're paying . . . "

"Jesus," Parker said. "What's got into you today?"

Wilson bounced like a monkey, scratching under both armpits. "Or, or. Grick. Grick."

"This is what happens when he gets to bed early," Parker said to Patrick. Mrs. Van Slyke returned.

"Parker?" He rose to his feet balancing his coffee, assumed a good humored expression, and approached Mrs. Van Slyke.

"Her husband's a bad dude," Wilson said. "Nothing you couldn't handle." His live eye gleamed. "He did a good painting of a boxer, once. They got married."

"He married the boxer?"

"Smart ass." Wilson shook his head. "Then he slowed down—know what I mean?" They considered Mrs. Van Slyke who had Parker more or less pinned against the lilacs. "My woman gets in the way . . . " He snorted. "I don't even have a studio, paint right in the living room."

"You a painter?"

"All the time, man. What do you do?"

"Read a lot—science. Trying to find out what's true about things."

"I'll tell you one truth," Wilson said. "It don't count until it's on the wall." He leaped back on his ladder and attacked peeling paint, banging his scraper on the siding to keep time. Sweat dripped into a bandanna rolled and tied around his forehead. Patrick got to work.

At four-thirty, Wilson gave him a ride home. Patrick washed and walked into town where he had a few beers and talked about the war with a guy named Wendell, a guy named Joe , and Willow, the friend of Amber's. He left early and slept well.

The week passed quickly. On Friday afternoon he cashed his first check at the Bank of Orange and Ulster County and walked over to the Depresso.

"Hey Patrick."

"Sam. Hot one." Sam worked for Parker on another job; he was part of the morning gathering at the News Shop.

"How you getting along with Willy?"

"Good."

"Crazy bastard," Sam said. "He was in Korea; his father or grandfather was a general or something."

"My father's in the Army."

"No shit. Yeah, well, Willy—his job was to go out and bring back North Koreans for the intelligence guys. Told me they went out at night. Said the North Koreans were supposed to be alive, but it was easier if they were dead."

"No wonder he's crazy. Hey, Claude."

"What's happening, Patrick?"

"I got paid."

"Don't tell him that," Sam said.

"Mon ami . . . "

"Hi, Claude." A young woman stepped next to Claude and took his arm.

"Who's your friend?" she asked, looking at Patrick.

"This is Patrick."

He remembered her gray eyes; she was the one who had smiled at him on his first night in town. Up close, he noticed tiny freckles and a gap between her front teeth.

"I'm Sue," she said.

"Hi."

"Claude is a famous ski jumper, did you know?" She was grinning widely.

"You ski, Patrick?" Claude asked.

"A little."

"I'm from the U.P., did 300 feet at Iron Mountain."

"Yo!"

"No more. Now I go one time a year to the Bear Mountain meet. Little jump."

"You won last year," Sue said.

"Year before, Cher."

"Claude, have you seen Jim?"

"Not today."

She frowned. "Bye, Claude. Bye, Patrick." Patrick watched her leave.

"So who's Jim?" he asked.

"Her boyfriend—alcoholic dude, a nice guy. She likes you." Claude drifted along the bar; he knew everyone. Patrick was beginning to feel at home in the Depresso. Amber had come in twice during the week, once with Willow and once with a builder named Art. She had smiled at Patrick, but she wasn't available—although her smile seemed to indicate that any day she might be. I'm on her list, Patrick thought, smiling back.

He finished the Darwin book and started *An Introduction to Mathematics* by Alfred North Whitehead. One evening in the Depresso, Sue came over to his table and asked what he was reading. "Listen to this," he said.

"Operations of thought are like cavalry charges in battle: they are strictly limited in number; they require fresh horses; they must be made only at decisive moments."

Sue wrinkled her nose. "Too much." She sat down.

"I mean, this book is a classic. What is math, anyway? Right here," Patrick said, patting the cover. "Lays it out. You can learn anything you want from books."

"Why aren't you in school somewhere?"

"I was; I quit. It was just a place where they put you in a box—a lawyer box, a doctor box. I didn't want to be in a box. Besides, it was expensive." Sue giggled.

"So, where are you from, Sue?"

"Michigan, same as Claude—except he's from the U.P."

"What are you doing in Woodstock?"

"Art Students League. I model and take classes."

"Should have known," Patrick said, "everyone I meet is an artist."

"You seen Jim: tall, cute?"

"I don't think so."

"He's a reader, too. He gets a pile of books and a six-pack, lies on the couch and reads all day." She looked around and sighed. "Later, Patrick." She left, relaxed and alert, like a fox on the move.

The next night she sat at his table again. "It's hot," she said.

"Want a beer?"

"No thanks."

"I get thirsty staring at white all day," Patrick said.

"You want to go swimming?"

"Sure." Patrick surprised himself. "Where?"

"I know a place."

"I don't have a car."

"I've got my roommate's for the night."

When they got into the car, Sue twisted and reached past Patrick to arrange something on the back seat behind him. She was sweating slightly, and he was astonished by her sweet rich smell. "That's strange," he said, "we've got the same smell. How can that be? Same genes? I'm mostly Irish. What are you?"

"Half Polish, half Ojibwa," she said. She drove to Shady and followed the Sawkill creek to a spot where she could pull off the road. She led Patrick through trees and down a steep path to the stream. It was nearly dark as they walked over rocks to a bend where a deeper pool curved along the outer bank. Sue crossed below the pool to a shingle of rocks and boulders and kicked off her sandals. "Here," she said.

Patrick noticed the orange glow of cigarettes on the opposite bank, but he couldn't see the faces behind them. He forgot about them when Sue pulled her T-shirt up over her head and stepped out of her jeans and underwear. "C'mon, Patrick." Her body was compact and tanned; one curve flowed naturally into the next. He stripped awkwardly, thinking that there was a first time for everything, and followed her into the icy water. She swam up and down, diving and surfacing, blowing water, black hair sleek behind her ears. Patrick did a few somersaults and floated, feeling the heat of the day drain out of his body.

"Oooh," she said, walking out of the water and onto the rocks. "Let's build a fire." They broke dead branches, took a few pages from Patrick's pocket notebook, and started the fire with her lighter. Patrick stood in front of the small blaze; Sue sat on her jeans, her knees drawn up to her breasts.

"Hey TURD face. Where d'ja come from? UNDER A FUCKING ROCK?" Patrick spun around. He saw a white face in the dark, a man standing behind a low line of boulders, fifteen feet away. "FUCKING IDIOT?" The man's voice was twisted, nearly screaming; his eyes were distorted. He was beefy, too big to mess with. "FUCKING QUEER!" He took a step forward. Patrick became oddly calm. There was a rock by his ankle, the size of a grapefruit. He slowly flexed his knees and looked into the man's eyes. Scoop the rock and smash his face, one motion. The man yelled again. Patrick held his eyes. Time slowed. A stick snapped behind Patrick, and the hair rose on the back of his neck. Sue hadn't moved. He was trapped. He didn't dare turn his head.

"Let's get the hell out of here," a voice said behind him.

"Fuck him, let's get out of here, go get a beer."

"He's an asshole!"

"Yeah, fuck him, let's go get a beer."

The white face hesitated and turned away. The two crashed through the woods, swearing and shouting.

Patrick put his clothes on as fast as he could. "I was going to kill him," he said, in shock. "I mean, I knew how. It was already in me." Sue smiled. "Get dressed, Sue! What if they come back?" She got to her feet and stood naked on the rocks as though she were in her bedroom, firelight flickering up her body.

He put out the fire while she dressed. His heart was still pounding as they climbed up the bank and walked quickly to the car. "Did you see the other guy?"

"He was in the dark," Sue said. "I couldn't see him."

"He sounded local," Patrick said. "He saved the scene. That guy was flipped out, gone! Sounded like he was from North Carolina or some place down there. He was gone."

It was a relief to be on the road.

"I need a beer," he said when they reached town.

"O.K., Patrick, see you," Sue said, stopping in front of the Depresso.

"O.K." He paused. "You are really beautiful." She made a wry smile that said, "I already know that."

"Night, Patrick."

The next day, during coffee break, he told Wilson what had happened. "Chicks," Wilson said.

"I never knew I could kill somebody," Patrick said. "I mean— I'm not the violent type. But it was all inside me, like it was pre-wired or something. I never looked at that rock, but I knew it was there."

Wilson sighed. "Knife comes in handy sometimes," he said. Patrick took a folding Opinel out of his pocket. "Too small,"

Wilson said. His hand brushed the black handle of the hunting knife he wore on his belt. "Bad shit," he said. He stood up. "Gotta put the paint on the wall, Patrick."

That night, Sue did not show up at the Depresso. A week later, she came into the bar with Jim, laughing and having a good time. She waved at Patrick like an old friend, but she didn't say anything to him. He felt less isolated, seeing her. He hadn't touched her, but he knew her smell and what she looked like underneath those clothes.

On Saturday, Parker invited him to a party at his house. When Patrick arrived, the downstairs was full of people talking loudly and drinking steadily. He learned that Parker, too, was a drop out—from Harvard—and that the Mercedes had belonged to his mother. "You know," Patrick said to him after a few beers, "when people talk, I get the feeling I'm missing something. It's like they're saying one thing but really talking about something else. It's like there's another layer underneath everything."

"You're learning," Parker said. Desperation crossed his face. He looked as though he might get in his car and drive away forever. Instead, he smiled helplessly and went for another drink. Patrick met Wilson's wife, Elaine, a short cheerful woman with a plain face and an extravagant body. Wilson was making pronouncements about the paintings on Parker's walls, mentioning painters Patrick had never heard of. Parker's two sons were running about having a great time. Parker and his wife, Hildy, were both stout blondes with fair complexions and blue eyes. Their boys were stamped from the same mold. Patrick could see them someday hauling ladders, driving elegant old cars, and charming well-to-do housewives.

Joe Burke showed up and introduced Patrick to his lady. "Sally Daffodil," he called her. She was tall and athletic with a grace and coloring that was like the flower. They were a good pair, Patrick thought, funny and open, yet . . . He sensed reserves in them that ran deep.

Patrick wasn't used to the company of so many sharp people in one room. Gino Canzoni came in, the foreman of Parker's other, larger, crew. He was tall and ironic. He had a rep on the crew for fearlessness at great heights. "My wife, Cree," he said to Patrick. She was dark with slender intelligent features. She had a blinding smile. The charm and pain and hint of wildness in her smile obliterated Patrick's defenses.

"Hi," he said. She accepted his surrender.

"Welcome to town," she said gaily. He felt included. Gino and Joe had grown up in Woodstock and were old friends. The group stood around telling stories. "Before Gino took me to meet his family," Cree said, "he told his mother that he had fallen for an older woman from the Midwest."

"Give her something to worry about," Gino said.

"Six months," she laughed.

"Funny thing was," Gino went on, "the same week that Cree was meeting everybody, Vassar degree and all that, she was on display at the checkout counter in the Grand Union—on the cover of Modern Detective."

"A gun to my head," Cree said. "Forced to open a safe."

"Leg shot," Gino said proudly. Sally Daffodil smiled patiently. Joe looked a bit restless.

"Are you a model?" Patrick asked.

"Was," Cree said and led Sally away. Parker put on a Dixieland album. Vassar? Gino was a Dartmouth graduate. Joe Burke was doing carpentry work but had dropped out of Hamilton College. He and Gino were writers of some kind. Patrick felt that he had stumbled into an alternative world; the more educated you were, the less money you made, or something. He didn't understand this world. It attracted him and put him off. It was free in a way that seemed good. But it was threatening, somehow. There was something overripe about it. He went outside and had a non-alternative hamburger, served to him by the older boy. The smell of meat cooking on the grill was delicious. Smoke rose, drawing Patrick's eyes up the dark green mountain to the ridge line, an hour's walk above them.

"So, how do you like our fair town?" Hildy asked.

"Very fair it is," Patrick said. "Good burger!"

"Plenty more where that came from." Patrick heard a trace of Europe in her voice.

"Are you from Woodstock?"

"I was born in the Netherlands," she said. "We came over not long after the war."

"I used to live in Germany," Patrick said. "Very different."

"Ja," Hildy said and yelled at Alden, the youngest, to get away from the road. She turned back to Patrick.

"What brings you to Woodstock?"

"I heard it was an interesting place. My father lived here for a couple of years, once."

"There are a lot of artists," Hildy said. "Musicians, too. And writers. They're all artists, I guess. Parker likes having people on his crew he can talk to. Are you a painter?"

"Nope. I'm not anything yet."

Hildy looked at him. "Hmmm," she said. "I'm a mother. And a cook."

"I think I could learn to cook," Patrick said.

"Sure you could; it just takes practice—and you have to love it. That's the secret ingredient. You have to love it. ALDEN!"

Patrick finished his burger, thanked Parker and Hildy, and walked down the road. As the sounds of the party faded behind him, he began to relax. He hadn't realized how tense he'd been. What's the matter with you? he asked himself. Parties are for fun, right? But he had to admit that it hadn't been fun, not really. Interesting, but not fun. What is fun? Is it when you don't care what happens?

He turned down Rock City Road toward town. If you didn't care at all, you wouldn't be interested in what happened; it wouldn't matter. How could that be fun? But, if you cared a lot, you would be too tense to have fun. I guess, he thought, you have to care a little, enough to be interested, but not too much. He tended to be on or off; he cared intensely or he didn't care at all. In this case, he thought, he cared too much. He wanted a woman. He was just as good as Joe Burke or Gino Canzoni. They had women. Beauties. They were citizens or writers or artists or whatever they were. Who was he?

Patrick couldn't answer that question. He just knew that he was as good as they were. That meant that somehow, someday, he would show up at a party with someone like Amber and make jokes and have fun. This was a cheerful thought. But, in the meantime, he had to learn more science. And art—what the hell was art all about? By the time he reached town, Patrick was singing songs from a Burl Ives record that his mother used to play when Patrick was a little boy. *"How can there be a cherry that has no stone? How can there be a baby with no cryin'?"*

Chapter 4

Willow lifted groceries from the bicycle basket, took them inside, and set them on the counter with a satisfying thump. Onions, garlic, a green pepper, a red pepper, basil, a can of coconut milk, a can of chicken stock, a small can of curry paste, chicken, lettuce, and two bottles of Gewurztraminer. The wine was extravagant. No doubt about that. But, for once it was her money. Ann had given her a job mornings at the Deli. Willow took her first pay directly to the Grand Union supermarket. She had been to the library and copied a recipe for curry and the name of the recommended wine. She put the wine in the refrigerator. Amber owed Art a meal, and Willow had volunteered to cook.

It was two in the afternoon, warm, too early to start. She was tempted to lie down and read, but instead she took a straw hat from a peg by the door and walked outside. Bees were buzzing in the roses. The tops of the trees were dark against a bright blue sky. Her feet led her into the pine woods on the far side of the studio where a deep layer of pine needles softened her steps. She walked for five minutes and stopped. In the distance, a chainsaw snarled twice and was silent. The air was still and resinous. Small sounds filtered through the branches above her. A young chickadee flew toward her, pausing briefly on low branches. Willow remained motionless. The tiny black and white bird hopped and flew directly to her shoulder. She felt its thin claws shift as its head turned first one way, then the other. It rested a moment as Willow filled with a mixture of elation and deep humility. A quick whirring of wings and the chickadee was ten yards farther on its way.

Willow remained still, her eyes misty, her mouth slightly open. She let the special feeling spread through to her fingertips and the soles of her feet. No words for this, she thought. As if in answer, the chickadee called. That's it, Willow said to herself—two notes descending, a major third. She repeated the two notes in her mind. The call and the feeling and the quiet beating of her heart wove together like a shawl to be saved for the future. Hers. Her.

"God," she said. She was thirsty. She continued slowly through the woods, working her way downhill. At some point she would meet the lower road, and she could walk back to the beginning of AhnRee's driveway. She came to the top of a ledge which she followed until she found a place to scramble down. At the base of the ledge, she straightened and listened. Banjo notes were picking their way through the trees. An easy deliberate rhythm drew her along and down the hill, farther from AhnRee's drive. The notes grew louder. Willow could see a clearing and part of a roof line through the trees. Someone was playing in the back yard.

She paused. The player was practicing "Cripple Creek," getting into it further and further. My day for music, she thought. When it stopped, she clapped with pleasure and emerged from the trees onto a rough lawn. The banjo player was sitting under a birch tree on a wooden kitchen chair. "Right on! Excuse me," she said, "I was walking and I stopped to listen. Where am I?"

"Cripple Creek," he said and smiled. "My back yard. My mother's, actually." He was tall and thin with shoulder length reddish hair and a wispy mustache that was supposed to make him look older. His hands were large. Long fingers wrapped around the neck of the banjo he was holding upright on his lap.

"I'm Willow. I live up there in AhnRee's studio," She pointed up the mountain.

"Ah, yes—AhnRee. I'm Martin. Lower Byrdcliffe Road is just down at the end of the driveway." Willow couldn't decide whether he was shy or busy. He seemed to be telling her to hoof it. The Devil made me do it, that's what she told Amber later.

"I can play Cripple Creek.

"Oh yeah?" He held the banjo toward her.

"Not on that. Do you have a violin, umm, fiddle?"

"Strangely enough . . . " He stood up, leaned the banjo against the chair, and said, "Be right back." Now what have I done? Willow asked herself. She hadn't touched a violin in two years. He brought her an old violin, nothing special, but the strings and the bow were in good shape. She played a few notes.

"Been a while," she said. She played the first bars of *Cripple Creek*. Such an easy melody. It sounded horrible. She stopped. "Just a second." She took two deep breaths and let the feel come back to her. She played one long slow note, listening. Better. She played the note again. She played two notes. Her body began to wake up. It was surprising how you played the violin with your whole body. I mean, God, she'd been playing since she was three. She began again, more slowly. She had now forgotten Martin. She played it through. Then again, a little faster. Yes, she thought, and took it at a tempo close to the one she'd heard through the trees. Halfway through, she heard a few tentative notes from the banjo. She smiled, eased back, and let Martin lead. They played until they had managed a decent version and stopped. There was another burst of applause. A woman with short blonde hair and a heart shaped face was clapping by the corner of the house.

"Hi, Mom. This is my mother, Heidi, ah, Willow."

"How do you do," his mother said. "Very nice."

"Willow appeared out of the woods," Martin said.

"Ah," his mother said, "a wood nymph. This is the time of year. Although, I must say, musical wood nymphs are rare."

"Well," Willow said, handing the violin and bow to Martin, "I'm off to gather mushrooms, back to my dwelling of twigs and pine cones." She smiled at Martin's mother, the pretty bitch, and walked into the woods without looking back, damned if she was going to go down their driveway. A few moments later, she heard *Cripple Creek*, as if in apology. Or was he just going back to work?

There was something familiar about Martin, an intangible set to his attitude, a stubbornness. She thought back over her friends but couldn't come up with the match. Memory is strange, she thought. It's all in there, but you lose the keys, the entry ways. It's like a city that keeps growing and growing. I mean, you have to go back and back to the old neighborhoods? Lennie Rosenbloom, Mr. Rosenbloom to her, encouraging but firm as she struggled through that Mozart sonata, his hurt smile directing her to feel the music—he was shorter than Martin and his hair was sandy colored. God, the light on his neck and chest. She was 13, so close to blushing all the time that she had to act like a zombie to keep herself under control. Played like one, too. God. No, it wasn't Mr. Rosenbloom. The road appeared beyond a clump of bushes. She pushed through and turned toward AhnRee's.

She had walked farther than she thought. By the time she reached the driveway, she was worrying about dinner. She planned as she hurried up the hill toward the studio: first, the onions and the peppers, get them going in the large cast iron frying pan; second, the chicken, cut in chunks; then the chicken stock and the coconut milk, the curry and the basil. Whoops, forgot the rice. Start that right after the onions and the peppers; give it time to steam a little and not be so wet. She placed the straw hat on its peg, drank a large glass of water, and played "*Highway 61 Revisited.*"

"*Like a rolling stone . . .* " she sang along as she cut up onions. "*To be on your own . . .* " Whack, whack. "*How does it feel? . . .* " Whack, whack. Amber and Art arrived in the middle of "*Desolation Row.*"

"Listen to that," she said as Bob Dylan's harmonica blew out the pain and isolation.

"Damn," Art said, "that smells good."

"Listen!" Willow said, turning up the volume.

"*Don't send me no more letters, no—not unless you mail them from Desolation Row.*" Dylan's intensity, the smell of curry, Amber's perfect body next to Art's shoulders, and her own unnamed passion coalesced into another moment she would never forget. "Too much," she said when the piece ended. "Want some wine?" She busied herself with dinner. Earlier, with the chickadee on her shoulder, she was a child of the universe. Now, she felt reborn as an adult. It was so lonely and sad, so—terminal.

She looked at Amber and Art. They did not appear to be in crisis. Art was lighting up a joint. Willow took a few hits out of politeness. She didn't mind getting high once in awhile, but the smoke in her lungs felt foreign and unhealthy. Amber, who smoked cigarettes occasionally, dragged away with gusto, the little pothead. Art was following her around with his eyes as though he were chained.

She served and poured; they ate and drank. The evening got blurry. Willow told them about the chickadee and about playing *Cripple Creek.*

"Yeah," Art said. "He lives in a house behind his mother's. She's got money, or the family does. Don't know much about

Martin; he went to private school, was only around summers. His father was a pilot. He died about ten years ago."

"He plays banjo pretty well," Willow said.

"Yeah, I guess. How come you stopped playing the violin?"

Willow scratched one knee. "I love the old greats," she said. "I mean they are great souls, but . . . "

"They weren't your soul," Art said.

"No. I mean, they are, but they aren't." She put her hands behind her head into her hair and paused, spreading her arms out slowly, letting long dark strands run through her fingers and fan across her shoulders. She shook her head. "I didn't want to be stuck in that scene forever. Doors were closing."

"Willow's father is a music prof," Amber said.

"My mother plays, too," Willow said. "A nice Jewish musical family with perfect children who know how to get along."

"What's wrong with getting along?" Amber smiled meaningfully in Art's direction.

"Maybe you could sing; you look a little like Joan Baez." Art was a decent guy, really. And he had those shoulders. Willow's ears were buzzing.

"I wish," she said.

"You got any Coltrane?" The guy was full of surprises.

"We do." She rose slowly and flipped through the albums that Amber had borrowed from AhnRee. "Night music," she said, putting it on the stereo. Amber was smiling broadly and wiggling her toes.

"Ice cream," she said. Willow remembered that she had to work in the morning.

"Bedtime for me," she said. Amber promised to do the dishes.

"Great dinner," Art said.

She closed the porch door behind her and stepped out of her clothes, feeling the cool night air on her skin. She stretched,

reaching high with her fingers, and then slid her hands apprais-
ingly down her sides and hips. This feeling of aloneness, this
new sense of herself, wasn't so bad. Whatever it was, it was real.
She pulled a blue broadcloth nightshirt over her head and lay in
bed, drifting away from the muffled tenor sax, out toward the
trees and the summer night. The quiet lured her, not so much
for itself, although it was wonderful, but for what might arise
within it.

In the morning, Art's truck was gone; Amber was nowhere
to be seen; and the dishes were dry, upside down in neat piles.
Willow ate a bowl of cold cereal with milk and then rode into
town. The first thing she did at Ann's was to make a pot of
coffee. Drinking too much wine gave her a headache, but dope
left her head filled with a dull cloudiness that drove her nuts. It
didn't hurt, but she couldn't think. It was as if she'd watched a
dumb television show all night. "Dumb, dumb, dumb," she sang.
"I'm dumb, dumb, dumb-deedoo-dumb, dumb, dumb. Where's
my bass man?" she asked the coffee pot. "There we go," she
said as coffee began running into the Silex pot. "Dumb, dumb,
deedoo."

"So it's a canary I hired?"

"Tweet. What are you doing up?"

"Couldn't sleep—smelled the coffee. We had a late delivery;
see if you can get the stuff out before it gets busy."

"Tweet, tweet." Ann acted grumpy, was grumpy, especially
early in the day, but there was no edge to it. The feeling was
directed more at herself. Willow did what she was told without resentment, agreeing with Ann's pronouncements whenever
possible. Ann wasn't around that much. The whole idea was
that Willow would open the Deli and let her sleep.

Ann took a cup of coffee upstairs, grumbling about the Pentagon and Johnson's war. Willow began pricing cans of deli-
cacies. Stocking was easy; it was the little price stickers that

slowed her down.

She was in the back room, looking down into a carton, when a voice called out, "Anybody home?" She saw a familiar head of red hair. Patrick, she realized as she came to the front of the store.

"Hi, I was in the back." Now that was intelligent, she thought. Patrick was considering the meat and cheese on display in the counter cooler. "Is it Patrick?" Brilliant. He straightened and turned.

"Himself," he said. "Good morning, Willow. What are you doing here?"

"Working, natch." She saw him start to grin; probably he thought she was a little rich girl.

"Oh," he said. "Could you make me a roast beef sandwich? To go?"

"White, wheat, pumpernickel, light rye, dark rye? . . . "

"Dark rye."

"You want some horseradish in there? Mayo? What?" Patrick rubbed his chin.

"Hell of a decision," he said. He turned his face up to the universe for guidance. "Horseradish?"

"Horseradish," she said firmly. "And a little mayo on the other side. I'll wrap the pickle separately, so it won't get soggy."

"Pickles are supposed to be soggy." He was grinning again.

"The sandwich, Patrick."

"Ah." He was altogether pleased with himself. She made the sandwich, mumbling like a junior Ann, and at the last moment included an extra pickle.

"There," she said. As he gave her a five dollar bill, the edge of his palm brushed her fingers. She put the change on the counter between them, not wanting to touch him again; she was still feeling his hand, pleasantly hard against hers, and she wanted to go on enjoying it. "Off you go," she said.

"Gotta put the paint on the wall. That's what Wilson says." He took the bag and the change. "Maybe I'll see you and Amber at the Depresso." Damn him.

"Maybe." She gave him her best Mona Lisa smile and flicked some hair back over her shoulder. A horn honked.

"Speaking of Wilson . . . " he said. "Thanks."

He's cute, she thought. Her hand was still warm where he had touched her. Like the ocean, his eyes darkened, the deeper she looked.

The next morning, Patrick was back. "Good sandwich," he said. He meant it, and she felt a warm stirring. God, not a blush!

"Let's do that again." She hadn't wanted him to think of her as a useless rich girl; now she didn't want to be Mother Earth. She opened her mouth to speak and closed it. Confusing. Fortunately, he had turned to the drinks cooler. She made the sandwich, including the extra pickle, and took his money from the counter. As she reached toward him with the change, her arm dipped and her hand rested for a moment on his palm. "Thanks, Willow. Have to run."

"Bye." He was out the door and into an old blue pickup before she could think of anything else to say. It wasn't me, she thought. I didn't do that. It was my arm, like a damned dowsing rod.

Two guys came in for coffee and bagels. A steady flow of customers kept her occupied; by noon she was over the embarrassment. But she was on alert. At dinner she said to Amber, "My goddamn arm was out of control." Amber clapped. "Oh, great," Willow said. "I'm groping strangers, and you think everything's fine."

"It is fine. You just need to get laid, that's all. And how can you call Patrick a stranger? You've known him for a month."

"Get laid—that's your solution for everything."

"No, no. It's a help; it takes the pressure off. And it's interesting, Willow. Men are so different. Now, we're not talking babies, here." Amber took a bite of bread. "Mmm, this bread . . . " She swallowed. "Yumm. You're getting it; those first couple of loaves were kind of a workout. You could get some good men, Willow; they're around. You need a strategy."

"I'll pass out numbers at the News Shop," Willow said.

Amber laughed. "Give number one to Patrick. Maybe number two to that cute Claude. Leave Art out; I'm not done with him. He's got a lot of talent, Willow. You know what he told me last night?"

"Let's see . . . "

"He's buying another old barn—for its frame. He's going to put the frame against his house barn, end-to-end. He wants to roof it and hang one room in a quarter of the upper level, leaving the rest open. Can't you see them: the finished barn and the design together, sort of turning into each other?"

"Neat idea," Willow said. "O.K., I'll leave Art out."

"Oh, I forgot to tell you," Amber said. "There's a big party, Saturday night. It's going to be on the mountain at a place called, `Mead's Meadow.' Art says they have it every year. It goes on all night; some people bring sleeping bags. Kegs, music—why don't you ride up with us?"

"Maybe I will," Willow said. "If I have any numbers left."

Chapter 5

Patrick held the brush handle between his palms and walked to the middle of the Van Slyke's lawn, rubbing his hands back and forth, spinning the brush until it was dry. "See if you can finish the garage by four," Parker had said. Good deal, it couldn't be later than three. The paint cans were stacked by the ladder and the folded drop cloths. He put the brush on top of the cans, took the rag and the putty knife out of his back pockets, and stepped back. Amazing how much better a paint job looks from twenty feet away, he thought.

"Looks good," Hendrik said from the kitchen door.

"Yes," Patrick said.

"Where your wheels?"

"Parker's going to pick me up."

"Have a beer while you wait?"

"Excellent," Patrick said. Hendrik went into the kitchen and reappeared with two bottles of Heineken. He waved Patrick over to a picnic table and opened the bottles with a pocket knife. He was a strong man with a brooding expression and a flattened nose. He looked like someone who might have painted a famous picture of a boxer. "Happy days," Hendrik said.

"Prosit." There are few things better than the first swallow of cold beer after a day's work. "Yes!" Patrick said.

"Looks good," Hendrik repeated. "Have to keep after these old houses."

"You've got a nice one. Is that your studio over there?"

"Yep."

"Could I ask you a question?"

"Sure."

"What is art, anyway?" Hendrik raised his eyebrows. He took several long swallows of Heineken. "I've met a lot of artists in this town," Patrick went on, "and I realized that I don't understand it."

"Bunch of bullshit, mostly."

Patrick waited. Hendrik looked at him and sighed. He took another swallow of Heineken and indicated the valley with one hand. "Everybody wants to be an artist," he said. "Doctors. I saw a clinic the other day—said `Medical Arts Group' on the building." He burped. "It's like this, Patrick: there's art, capital A—fine art, it's called sometimes—and there's everything else."

"So what is this `fine art?'"

Hendrik shook his head. He went into the house and came out with two more beers. "Let's start with everything else," he said. "It's easier." He pried off the bottle caps. "Everything else is commercial art—calendar graphics or posters or paintings of lighthouses, fall foliage, the streets of Paris—that kind of stuff, done in familiar styles. Nothing wrong with it. But it isn't art; it's craft." He drank. "It's craft because the painters know what they're doing when they start. Some of the paintings seem magical, but it's trick magic. They know how to get the rabbit out of the hat. An artist—capital A—doesn't know what's in the hat or how to get it out."

"Hmm," Patrick said.

"A guy in Vermont came up with that comparison—Robert Francis. It's like this, Patrick: an artist needs to make a picture that expresses how he feels about something or someone or some place. Since every artist is different, good paintings, true paintings, are original."

"True?"

"Yeah, true to the artist's feelings," Hendrik said.

"True," Patrick said, turning the word over in his mind.

"It's not so easy. What the hell, I'll show you." Hendrik got up and led Patrick to his studio.

"Look there," he said, pointing at a wall covered with charcoal drawings of a nude Julie Van Slyke, fifteen years younger. "Those are studies I made before I did the painting. You can see how I kept circling around the central idea, this line here." He moved one hand through the air as though he were stroking her hip. "Once I got it right, it was mostly a matter of color. Not a bad painting, as it turned out."

Patrick saw what Hendrik meant through a light haze of embarrassment. He took a drink from his bottle of Heineken and acted grown up. Mrs. Van Slyke was leaning forward. She had unexpectedly exotic breasts that hung and then swelled upwards. "The thing is, it can take a while before you get it. Sometimes you never get it. I've been working on this one all year." Hendrik walked over to a heavy wooden easel. A canvas, half painted, half sketched in pencil, showed a young man sitting by a fireplace and holding a guitar. His chair was sideways to the fire. His body and guitar were turned toward the painter. There was a wine bottle on the floor next to the chair.

"No glass," Patrick said.

"He's drinking alone."

"Why is he turned? Who is he looking at?"

"Maybe if I knew that, I could paint the goddamned thing."

"Oh," Patrick said. "I like it—so far, anyway. Pretty intense."

"Hendrik, are you there with Patrick?" Mrs. Van Slyke's voice came loudly through an intercom. Hendrik made a face, went over to the door, and pressed a plastic button.

"Yes, Dear."

"Parker is here for Patrick."

"Be right there," Hendrik said.

They walked side by side to the main house. Patrick felt himself looking at Mrs. Van Slyke differently; he was seeing her partly through Hendrik's eyes, as Hendrik had painted her. She was more female.

"Patrick asked what art is," Hendrik explained.

"Are you clear on that now?" Mrs. Van Slyke asked as she took the empty bottles from their hands. Parker was grinning on the sideline.

"Umm—it's over there," Patrick said, waving at the studio.

"Of course it is," Mrs. Van Slyke said without changing expression. "What wonderful crews you have, Parker! The place looks marvelous. I hope you will be able to do the studio next year."

"It will be first on on my list," Parker promised. "Come, Patrick, let's get the ladder on the rack."

"Thanks for the Heineken," Patrick said to Hendrik.

"Good job," Hendrik said.

"Goodbye, Patrick. I hope that we see you again." Mrs. Van Slyke smiled and waited for his reaction.

"Bye," he said. They hustled off. On their way down the mountain, he felt the mood lighten. "Whew," he said.

"Nice going, Patrick. A raise is in order—$2.25, retroactive to the beginning of this week."

"No shit!"

Parker slapped one knee. "It's over there—ha, ha—art . . . "

"Well it was, is," Patrick said.

"Yes, yes, no doubt."

Parker dropped him off at the Depresso. "Thanks for the raise."

"You earned it, Patrick. See you in the morning."

Patrick skipped down the stone steps to the Depresso patio. Willow was reading at a table, leaning back, her long legs stretched out before her, crossed at the ankles.

"Hey, Willow."

"Hello, Patrick. Hungry already?"

Patrick patted his stomach. "You make great sandwiches, but—I'm celebrating. I got a raise."

"Impressive," Willow said.

"I'll tell you about it, if you'd like. But I've got to get a beer. Want one?"

"No thanks."

Patrick returned with a Heineken, his new favorite. "Yeah, I finished a house and garage up on the mountain. The Van Slyke's. Do you know them?" Willow shook her head, no. "He's a painter, and she's a—looker. He showed me his studio. Do you know what art is, Willow?"

"God, Patrick," she said.

"What's the matter?"

"You ask the most amazing questions."

"Well, I asked Hendrik—Mr. Van Slyke—and he showed me his studio."

"Modest Hendrik."

"He was modest, in a frustrated way. He showed me a painting that he's been working on all year. Said he couldn't get it. He said that art had to be true."

"He didn't!" Willow clapped her hand over her mouth.

Patrick looked at her. "You think I'm a moron." She took her hand away. "I am. But I'm a persistent moron." He took a swallow of beer. "True," he said. "I know about true. In science, what is true can be verified. What is true, is true for everybody. But Hendrik's true is only true for Hendrik."

"Especially true for Hendrik," Willow said.

"So, it's a different kind of true," Patrick finished.

"Different from science," Willow said, "but useful."

"Useful . . . " Patrick thought.

"Like Beethoven or Dylan true," she said.

Patrick watched people on the sidewalk. "There's more," he said, after a moment. "There's more about this art and science stuff. I don't understand it, yet. What's the matter?" he asked for the second time. Willow was wiping tears from her cheeks.

"It's not your fault," she said. She stood suddenly. "I'm going now." She pedaled away with her book in the basket. What did I say? he wondered. He went inside scratching his head. Sue and Jim were at the bar. He thought about his usual dinner of rice and vegetables. To hell with it. Deanie's, he said to himself and went back outside. Willow was gone.

He walked past the News Shop and Ann's Deli and turned down the hill to Deanie's for a celebratory steak, still wondering what had upset Willow. The dining room was comfortably filled, cheerful without being noisy. A bar stretched the length of one end of the room. Sam was there by himself and said hello. Patrick excused himself as soon as he could and sat at a small table on the other side of the room. Sam was always mouthing off about the government and asking everyone where he could score some grass. He was nervous in a way that put Patrick off. Patrick didn't want to hassle with anyone who worked for Parker, so he kept his mouth shut and avoided him. "Meat," he said to Sam. "I've got this craving for meat. Got to have it!"

"Yeah, man." Sam's eyes darted around as Patrick escaped.

"Medium rare," Patrick ordered, and, by God, that's what he was served. Delicious. He ate slowly, each bite a mini-ceremony. Eating out was important to Patrick. While he was working, he worked hard, concentrating. Dinner was a time to relax, to think, and to look around. He enjoyed being in the midst of people without necessarily having to talk to anyone. The Deanie's crowd was straighter than the Depresso crowd. IBM'rs and local business people mixed with musicians and artists. The waitresses were middle-aged. The pies were particularly good.

This was Patrick's third dinner at Deanie's. He was beginning to feel more at home in Woodstock. His landlady, Gert, had become more friendly. Patrick was willing to help with little things around the house, that probably had something to do with it. She was a reader, too, he'd discovered. They talked about books. The other day, he'd asked her what she was reading.

"Every story is a love story, isn't it, Patrick?" She had chuckled comfortably and continued reading. He didn't know what to make of that. Did she mean every story about anything? Or every story a writer felt was worth the effort? She had said it as though it were self evident, as though he shouldn't be pestering her for an explanation. Or maybe he was supposed to figure it out for himself.

"Wonderful pie," he said to the waitress.

"We make a lot of them," she said. Patrick left a big tip and walked slowly toward home. He had an urge for a Hershey bar as he passed Ann's. Ann took his change without comment.

"Willow makes a good sandwich," he said.

"You like her, don't you," she said accusingly. He didn't know what to say. Ann glared at him. "You young people think we don't feel anything. Well, you're wrong. What's your name?"

"Patrick."

"We have feelings, too. You think we weren't young once?"

"Sorry," he said, unsure. "Night." He moved toward the door.

"Remember that, Patrick," she flung at his back. Another upset woman. What was getting into everybody? He looked into the window of the Depresso. Sue and Jim weren't there. The Go player who had annoyed him on his first night in town was sitting on a stool in a corner, playing a banjo. The metallic beat followed him a short distance up Tinker Street, a sort of urban bluegrass. It was a relief to go quietly to bed with his book on mathematics.

The next morning it was pouring. Patrick trudged to the News Shop, where Parker declared a washout. Gino, as senior man, got to work on an inside job. Everyone else was off for the day. The group milled around, joking with a drunk who kept coming in and out, clapping people on the back, breathing beer fumes in their faces, and saying, "How ya doing, buddy? How ya doing? That good, huh? Ha, ha, ha."

"Good to see you, Billy. Good to see you."

"So who's this?" he asked, putting one arm around Wilson and the other around Patrick.

"Patrick, Billy. This is Patrick."

"Top o' the mornin', Patrick." Patrick found himself laughing along with him.

"By Jesus," he said, "top o' the mornin' to you, too." They were leaving. Billy escorted them to the open doorway.

"Quack," he said, propelling them down the steps into the rain.

"Quack is right," Patrick said. "See you, Willy." Habit took him along the street to Ann's where he hesitated and then went in. "Hi, Willow. Rained out!"

Willow looked up. No one else was in the deli. "Patrick, I'm sorry I left so abruptly last night. I just couldn't . . . "

"That's O.K.; I won't talk about art anymore."

She smiled at him reprovingly.

"Anyway, I can't live without your sandwiches. How about turkey, today?" He stowed the sandwich in a small army surplus backpack that he'd bought after his first week in town.

"What are you going to do today?"

"I don't know," Patrick said. "Go to the library, I guess. I'm reading a great book on mathematics."

"There's supposed to be a party this weekend, Saturday, on the mountain. Mead's meadow, wherever that is. Music, kegs, a big blowout. Art says it's a good time. They do it every year."

"You going?"

"Yeah, for a while anyway."

"Maybe I'll see you there," Patrick said. "Day after tomorrow—the rain should be over by then." Willow seemed pleased, and Patrick left for the library. Hard to figure, he thought. Last night she wouldn't talk to me; this morning she invites me to a party. He thought he'd go, if he could find it. Maybe Art would fall off the mountain.

The library was pleasant and well lit. The science section was a bit out of date. There were many expensive art books locked in a big case. The children's room was large and cheerful with a painted wooden riding horse in one corner. He read for an hour and thought of writing to his parents, but he hadn't looked up his father's friend. He wanted to do that before he wrote, so he asked for a telephone book. Heidi Merrill was listed with an address on Lower Byrdcliffe Road. There was no pay phone in the library, so he walked over to the Woodstock Laundromat.

Joe Burke was folding clothes, standing at a counter beside a tall slender woman with long hair. She was teasing him about his folding. He leaned and said something softly in her ear that made her laugh. Her voice was low and appealing; it sounded to Patrick as though it had started in Texas and traveled around the world before it got to the laundromat. The energy between the two was intense and relaxed at the same time. Patrick stared.

"Hello, Patrick," Joe said, turning. "This is Daisy."

"Hello, Patrick," Daisy echoed. She looked at him with calm gray eyes and then picked up her basket of clothes. "Well . . . " she said.

"Onward," Joe said.

"Yes." Their eyes met, and she left, walking as though she were going slightly uphill. Patrick felt suddenly lonely.

"So, Patrick, what's happening?"

Patrick looked back from the door. "Oh. I'm trying to find someone named Heidi Merrill. Do you know where she lives?"

"Sure do, going right by there, if you want a lift." What the hell, Patrick thought, nothing else to do. It doesn't matter if she's home or not.

"Good deal."

They drove out of Library Lane, passing Billy at the entrance to Tinker Street. Joe rolled his window all the way open. "Hey, Billy. Want a lift?"

"Quack. You want me to miss my shower?"

As they drove through town, Patrick said, "I met him this morning in the News Shop. Quite a character."

"Yeah, we go way back," Joe said. "Used to take me pickerel fishing, Billy did—one of my heroes. He just got out of the slammer."

"What did he do?"

"One of the state cops, Dusty Rhodes, drove his cruiser into Billy's driveway to check him out for something or other, about three in the morning. The way Billy tells it, he woke up with a headache listening to a siren. He looked out his upstairs bedroom window. `That damn flashing light hurt my eyes,' Billy said. So he shot it out with a 30-30. Dusty arrested him for assault with a deadly weapon, and the judge asked him what he had to say for himself. `Your Honor,' Billy said, `Assault? Do you think if I'd wanted to hit Dusty, I'd have missed him?' The judge gave him six months."

"He seems like a good guy," Patrick said.

"He is. That's the Merrill's road, there."

Patrick thanked Joe and walked fifty yards through trees to a rambling house with clapboard siding stained brown. There was a second smaller house, or studio, some distance behind and to the right. A green Cadillac, at least ten years old, gleamed in front of the house. Patrick knocked on the screen door. A woman with a heart shaped face, wheat colored hair, and clear blue-green eyes answered his knock.

"Yes?"

"Good morning. Are you Heidi Merrill?" She nodded. "My name is Patrick O'Shaunessy." She straightened. "My father said that you were an old friend. He asked me to say hello for him and see how you're doing."

"Well! What a surprise. You must tell Brian that we are doing just fine. Come in." She led Patrick to a spacious kitchen where she poured coffee into hand-painted mugs. "So, Patrick, how long will you be in Woodstock?"

"Good question. I think until winter, at least—maybe longer. I like it here, so far."

"How long have you been here?"

"About a month."

"It is a nice town." A red '52 Chevy with a white convertible top drove past the kitchen. "Oh, there's Martin, my son. He lives in the studio behind the house." She looked at him closely. "You do remind me of Brian, but you must take after your mother. You're shorter, broader across the shoulders . . . "

"Yes, I guess I do."

"Same smile, though. How is Brian? You have a sister, don't you?"

"Yep, Molly, a year older than I am. She's married, living in Atlanta. Dad's fine. He's just about to retire from the Army. He and Mom are arguing about whether to live in Florida or Costa Rica. Heidi went over to the door where there was an intercom much like the Van Slyke's.

"Martin? Martin, can you come over? Patrick O'Shaunessy is here. His father is an old friend."

A voice crackled through the speaker, "O.K., just a minute."

Patrick looked around. "Nice house," he said.

"We've been here many years." There was a defensive note in her voice that surprised him. As he was telling her about his job, a tall man in his late twenties pushed open the kitchen door. He walked directly over, holding out his hand.

"Patrick O'Shaunessy?"

"Yes," Patrick said, standing and shaking hands.

"Martin Merrill."

"Patrick is working in town; he's not sure how long he will stay."

"What do think of the place?"

"The town, you mean?" Martin nodded. "I like Woodstock, but—everyone's a painter or a musician. Not that that's bad."

"And you are?"

"Martin, really!" Martin ignored his mother and stared at Patrick.

Questions didn't bother Patrick. He thought. "I don't know—scientist maybe, someday."

"Good deal. I don't know what I am either." Martin clapped his hands together and poured himself a cup of coffee. "But I'm working on it. Lot of good music around town, good musicians showing up. I've got a little recording studio in back."

"Do you play?"

"Very well," Heidi said.

"Not much," Martin said. "Fiddle. Banjo." Patrick imagined him playing the fiddle. He had large hands.

"My dad plays the fiddle." Martin was like a softer version of his dad, tall and thin. Heidi was watching him closely. He began to feel too warm. He rose to his feet. "Well, I'd better be going. It's been nice to meet you."

"Wait a minute," Martin said. "It's raining; I'll give you a ride."

"You just got here."

"No problem, I was just picking something up. I'll be back later this afternoon," he said to his mother.

"Goodbye, Patrick. I hope things work out for you. Do tell your father that everything's fine. And come and have dinner with us sometime, won't you?"

"That would be nice," Patrick said.

Martin dropped him at Gert's and wished him luck. "Oh, yeah," Patrick said as he was half out of the car. "Do you know where Mead's Meadow is?"

"Sure. It's near the top on the other side, after you pass the Mountain House. Right up Rock City Road, up and over. You go down a hill, and the road bends left. You'll see a little logging road on the right—goes down through the woods a little ways, across a wet spot, and up onto the meadow."

"Thanks." Patrick waved and watched him drive away. Neat car. He said hello to Gert and ate his sandwich on the porch, thinking hard. He started to write a letter to his parents, but he crumpled it after the first paragraph. He went inside. Gert was busy in the back of the house. He hesitated and then picked up the telephone and called home, collect. By good luck, his father answered. "Dad, this is Pat."

"Pat! Where are you?"

"I'm in Woodstock—great town. I just looked up Heidi and Martin Merrill."

"How are they?" His father's voice sounded far away.

"Fine. They've got a big place. She's nice, makes good coffee. Martin plays the fiddle." Patrick paused. "His hands, Dad, they are just like yours—like mine. He reminds me of you." Patrick ran out of words. There was a brief silence.

"It's a long story, Pat. I'll tell you about it the next time we get together. Martin is your half-brother."

Patrick let out his breath. "I was wondering. I didn't say anything."

His father was silent for a moment. "Maybe that's best, Pat. We wouldn't want to upset anybody; only a couple of people know. Come see us at Christmas in Costa Rica or Florida—wherever we end up; we'll talk about it. Basically, Heidi was afraid she'd never have a baby."

"Dad, look, I've got to go. Thanks for telling me. I won't say anything. I'll let you know about Christmas. Say hi to Mom." Patrick hung up softly. He stood for several seconds and then went back out on the porch where he sat down again and watched the rain. I'll be damned, he thought. His father must have been about his age when he was in Woodstock. Patrick saw him in a new way. Heidi must have been incredible; she was still good looking. It was cool to have a brother, but it was strange not to be able to say anything. Martin didn't seem like a bad guy for someone who had it easy.

"Patrick, the window at the end of the upstairs hall is stuck. Could you close it for me?"

"Glad to." Keep it quiet, he thought, climbing the stairs. Maybe talk about it at Christmas. See what happens.

Chapter 6

Willow followed Amber and Art across a small stream. "Much farther?" she asked. Art pointed through the trees to a small rise.

"Right up there." They emerged onto a shelf-like meadow that dropped abruptly into a narrow valley. Willow could see nothing but mountain after mountain in the distance—no roads, no houses. An upright piano stood by itself in the meadow, the last point of local focus before her eyes leaped into the space beyond and below.

"Wow!"

Amber and Art chose a place not far from a fire where a dozen people were sitting and standing, laughing, drinking beer. Willow removed her pack. She spread a blanket and weighed it down with the pack which held a bottle of water, two bottles of wine, a paperback copy of Lawrence Durrell's Justine, and a loaf of her best honey walnut bread. Art went immediately to the keg.

"Too much," Amber said, looking at the view.

"I wonder if Patrick will show," Willow said.

"Did you tell him where it was?"

"I didn't give him directions, but guys on his crew would

know."

"He'll come," Amber said. "And if he doesn't, that's his problem. How did they get the piano up here?" she asked Art who was back, holding three paper cups of beer.

"Carried it," he said. "Four guys—one on each corner. They bring it in every year. It's Angus's. He has a band, plays Dixieland and early jazz."

"Oooh," Willow said, "stride piano." She had grown up listening to Scott Joplin, Jelly Roll Morton, and Fats Waller, her father's nod to modernity. Straight from Bach, he used to say. She sipped her beer. Martin Merrill arrived.

"Hey there, Art. Hi, Willow."

"Hey, Martin. This is Amber. Where's your fiddle?"

"Hi, Amber. Fiddle's in the car. Maybe we'll get to a little Cripple Creek later." Willow flushed.

"I think I've retired," she said.

"Not allowed." Martin was having trouble keeping his eyes off Amber who had shifted to ground midway between a barnwarmer's dream and a folksinger's groupie. Here we go again, Willow thought.

"How's that Chevy running?" Art asked.

"Good. I just put new tires on her."

"That's a commitment. Love that car. Have you seen it, Amber—a red '52 convertible?"

"Not yet," she said.

God. Willow brought out the honey walnut loaf. "Anybody hungry?"

"Sure," Martin said. She broke off an end, the best part, and handed it to him.

"Good," he said, chewing.

"Willow can cook!" Art said. People were arriving steadily. It was five o'clock; the heat of the day was easing. A strong looking man in his thirties with a short beard and dark curly hair began to play the piano, his back straight.

"Yo, Angus!" someone called. Martin went for a refill and returned a few minutes later as Willow was looking around the meadow. She couldn't stop herself; every few minutes she checked again.

"Looking for someone?" Martin asked.

"Yeah, a guy I met—Patrick O'Shaunessy."

"Patrick O'Shaunessy?"

"Yes."

"I'll be damned. I met him the other day." Patrick, she thought. Martin reminded her of Patrick; that's who it was. More people arrived. A soprano sax joined the piano. A man with gray hair set up a drum kit. Joe Burke stood near the piano with a blonde—leggy, like me, Willow thought, but better looking. They came over and sat down. Joe introduced her, his wife, Sally. He reached into a paper bag and handed everyone a sparkler.

"It's the 4th," he said. They lit the sparklers and sat, more or less in a circle, waving them and drinking beer.

"My country 'tis of thee," Amber said.

"Old Glory," Martin added.

"Patriots!" A familiar voice. Patrick had come up behind her.

"Hey, Patrick." Martin stood, waved at Patrick, and wandered toward the kegs. Patrick sat down next to Willow. Joe handed him a sparkler. Willow leaned back on her elbows. The strains of *St. James Infirmary* and a heavy beat from the drummer mingled with the smell of burning sparklers and the sweeter smell of marijuana.

"It's good to be a citizen," Patrick said. Willow inspected him for signs of irony. None. They talked briefly about the war which they were all against. It seemed far away, a bad dream.

"Maybe we should get active," Patrick suggested, "demonstrate or something." Joe leaned forward.

"You want to watch it," he said.

"What do you mean?"

"I had kind of a shock last week," Joe said. "You know Ox?" He looked at the others.

"Sure," Art said.

"He was in school with us; he's a state trooper," Joe explained. "We've had narcs around for a few years now, busting people for the evil weed."

"Shit heads," Art said. "Like we really have a drug problem."

"We spot the narcs," Joe said. "Anyway, I was having a beer with Ox in Buckman's, and he told me to watch my ass. He told me there was a list of radicals at headquarters. Subversives. `They're watching you; that's all I can say.' " Joe shook his head. "I mean, I'm a veteran, for Christ's sake."

"You're a dropout," Art said.

Joe started to smile. "Look who's talking."

"So, who's watching?" Martin asked.

"Somebody is," Joe said. "Ox wouldn't have told me if he wasn't worried. FBI? CIA?"

"Martin's a commie pinko," Art said. "Is he on the list?"

"Should be," Joe said.

"What about Morgan? And Gino?"

"Subversives for sure. Down the Pentagon!" Joe raised his cup.

"Down the Pentagon!" echoed across the valley.

"O.K., Patrick," Amber said. "You can turn off the tape recorder." Patrick took a paper bag from his pack and held up a block of cheddar. He shook it by his ear.

"Wasn't on," he said.

"Might as well eat it, then," Sally said.

They ate and drank and wandered around the meadow. A washtub bass joined the music. Willow didn't exactly follow Patrick, but she managed to be in his general vicinity. She returned to her blanket and read until the light started to go. There was a book discussion. Patrick talked about a math book that he was reading, and Joe got started on significant digits, of all things. "You understand the principle," he said.

"Natch," Art said, "but here is Morgan, in case anyone needs a refresher." Willow tried to remember high school physics while she watched Morgan sit down deliberately. He had powerful shoulders and a sensitive expression. "Morgan, what are significant digits?"

"Ah," Morgan said, "the concept is that in scientific computation, the result cannot be more accurate than the least accurate quantity or measurement involved." There was light applause. Morgan drank deeply.

"Just so," said Joe. "And didn't I have a hell of a time understanding that? I thought you could make an answer as accurate as you wanted. You want seven decimal places? No problem." Patrick was sitting forward, listening intensely. "I finally got the idea, and I never forgot it," Joe went on. "Well, there I was in weather school in the Air Force, and their dew point calculation gave an answer that was more precise than one of the measurements. `These decimal points are meaningless,' I said to the sergeant. Yeah, right. Next thing you know, I'm in front of the base commander.

"`Burke,' he says, `you may have a point. But it's a goddamn small one. Are you an airman or a goddamn philosopher, Burke?'

"`Airman, SIR,' I said."

"Airman Burke," Art toasted.

Willow was impressed. She thought about Stanford—the academic cliques, the gorgeous football players, the socialites.

They were good at what they did; they were judged by how they performed in their groups; they lived by accepted rules. These people, in Mead's meadow, were just as sharp, just as physical (in a different way, maybe a better way), and just as easy and confident. They were all of the aboves. They were free. They were alive, or more alive, in a different way. A shiver ran up her back.

She opened a bottle of wine. The band was tighter, into *When the Saints Come Marching In*. As the light faded, the un-inhabited range of mountains before them became darker and more mysterious, unexpectedly comforting. The mountains were timeless, or in a different flow of time.

"This is what they saw," Patrick said, "the first people." He pointed across the valley.

"Do you want some wine?" She held up the bottle.

"Change of pace," he said. "Sure."

"Cabernet Sauvigon," she said with new authority. "Your basic meadow red."

The firelight cast shadows; the group seemed smaller and more vulnerable. "The first people . . . " Patrick repeated. They were the first people, now, she realized. She bit down on her lip. Her heart broke open like a swollen peach.

"There's a little bread left," she said. God, she was crying again.

"You cry a lot," he said.

"Oh, fuck you, Patrick." She poured herself more wine.

"I don't mind it," he said seriously.

"Look, do you want to go?" she asked.

"Sure." Amber was over by the band; she was staying all night or going over to Art's. Willow told her that she was leaving, and she and Patrick picked their way slowly through the woods. "I've got to get a little flashlight," Patrick said as they splashed across the stream.

When they came out onto the road, a patrol car was parked in the middle. Two cops were ticketing a long line of cars and trucks that were pulled off to the side. "What's the matter?" Willow asked.

"Blocking the road. Obstructing traffic."

"They are not. What traffic? This is the top of the mountain, for God's sake."

"You want to give us a hard time?" He was threatening. Patrick pulled her away.

"Let's go, Willow."

"Have you been drinking, lady? I wouldn't want to see you driving."

"We're walking." Willow glared at the cops and let Patrick guide her down the road. The band was working on a Dixie version of *America the Beautiful*; the sax floated high over the tree tops into the night. She looked back. One of the cops was answering a radio call; the other was still ticketing. They were trying to ruin everything. "Why, Patrick?"

"Groups," he said, after a moment. "Tribalism. They're afraid of change. When they get their backs up, Willow, you've got to work around them. If you challenge them, they get worse. It's weird, but the more powerful people are, the more frightened they are, usually. You'd think it would be the other way around."

"We've got to fight back," Willow said.

"We do—by existing." The starlight was sufficient for them to walk down the middle of the road. They were quiet and then they talked and then they were quiet again. One person, who had been at the party, stopped and offered a ride, but they decided to keep walking. Patrick told her about his parents and his sister, Molly. Nice people. She wondered where he got the hard edge she sensed beneath the surface. The Irish? Were his parents closet rebels? Maybe. Probably it was from hard

64

knocks. For what? From who? For being honest. That was it. From people who cut corners with the truth to get ahead or get along. They were the same that way.

At the bottom of the mountain, they turned down Reynold's Lane to Route 212 and then up the Glasco Turnpike to the Byrd-cliffe Road. At AhnRee's driveway, Willow said "Might as well walk me home."

"My mission," Patrick said. At the door, she suggested that they kill the bottle, and Patrick followed her in. She filled two glasses. They flopped into chairs at the kitchen table. She should have been exhausted, but she wasn't. When the wine was gone, Patrick stood. Before he spoke, she asked him for a hug, and before he answered she went to him and put her arms around his neck. His arms went uncertainly around her. She pressed the whole length of her body against him, molding her-self to his shape. His shoulders were broader than they looked. As his arms tightened, she felt herself loosen and grow warm. He took a deep breath. They were losing control. "Patrick," she said. "Patrick." She pulled away and took his hand. "Let's go out here." She led him to the porch and kicked off her shoes. Still holding his hand, she pulled him down onto the bed. She kissed him lightly with open lips. He was warm and tasted of wine and beer.

"My shoes," he said. She kissed him again, sliding her lips to the corners of his mouth and back. As he bent forward to take off his shoes, she unbuttoned her shirt and removed it. She stretched full length on the bed, naked to the waist, and held out her arms. She heard his quick intake of breath and felt his palm on her breast.

"Willow?" She pushed up against his hand and began to move slowly from side to side. There was no more thinking, only a rush of feeling. She pulled him into her and encouraged him to take her, fuck her, fill her with his hot hard energy. As he came and collapsed, she hugged him with her arms and her legs, surrounding him with warmth, keeping him safe.

She remained awake, savoring the moments. It was the right time of the month. No worries there. Her own need for orgasm was alive and well, like a promise. She stroked the back of his head, and he mumbled something in his sleep. God, they were together. She was still herself, but now she was something else, too. She had a pang of sadness for squirrelie, alone out there. Squirrelie.

She awoke snuggled against Patrick's back. She reached around and began to caress him. He was inside her before he was fully awake. She held him tightly, and as she began to peak she begged him not to stop. She was driving the train, and Patrick responded. "Baby," she called. "Ohhhh." She opened like an exploding flower. Another orgasm rolled through her, and then another and another. Completions. Irreversible. She cried in wonder and fell back as he came, adding to the warm flood in which she floated.

Some time later, she said, "The Big Bang Theory? I get it." Patrick rolled out of bed and dressed.

"I've got to go, Willow," he said.

She wanted him to stay. She wanted to make a good breakfast for them. She wanted to talk with him for hours, but a deeper voice, surprising her, said, "Bye, Patrick." He looked at her intently for a moment. "Bye, Patrick," she repeated softly.

Chapter 7

Patrick took a quick step and kicked a pebble into the woods along AhnRee's driveway. It would be fun to practice corner kicks again. Willow was intense. Nice, too. Dynamite in bed. Who would have thought it? He blasted another pebble between two trees. Goal! It was going to be hot later. Breakfast in the News Shop would be a good thing. Coffee. A fried egg sandwich. Willow's legs wrapped around him, and he relaxed for a moment remembering her hair against his cheek and over his shoulders where she had covered him. He felt a new sweetness inside. His head swam. "Too much," he said to the fans in the woods and ran twenty yards to wake up.

Billy Jakes slapped him on the back in the News Shop. "Long night, huh Patrick?"

"Long night, Billy." Just as well he didn't have to work today. He took a bite of his fried egg sandwich and thought about the first people and the view from Mead's Meadow. The green of the mountains was so fresh, empty as one of the new canvases stacked against Hendrik's studio wall. The first people had done well, really; they deserved a celebration. It was a righteous Fourth. Martin was there at first. Where had he gone? Patrick wanted to know more about him. The music was great.

And then those cops—they were really the losers, the ones left out or behind. Why did that have to be?

"Officer Allen, ha, ha, ha." Patrick turned and saw Billy put an arm around one of the cops who had been on the mountain, the larger one. "Gotta smoke? I'm innocent."

"Jesus, Billy. Here, Goddamn it."

"Obliged, Allen. I truly am." Billy took a deep drag.

"I see you drinking on the street, I'm going to lock you up."

"I am much obliged." Billy began to cough. He went outside, and Officer Allen waved his arm as if to clear the air. There was a polite silence punctuated by Billy's coughs which grew fainter as he moved down the sidewalk. Officer Allen left with a newspaper and a supply of Marlboros.

Gert was sitting on the porch when Patrick arrived home.

"Morning, Gert." She looked him over and smiled broadly.

"Good morning. I've a job for you, if you've a mind to do it."

"Well, I was going to work on the Unified Field Theory, but . . . " The Big Bang Theory. He started to smile and found himself turning red.

"Aren't we in a good mood," Gert said.

"What needs doing?"

"The attic. I've been cleaning, and I need some boxes brought down to the shed. They're too heavy for me." She led him up two flights of stairs and pointed out a group of boxes. "Fred is coming to haul them away some time next week. It's time to get rid of things."

"No problem. Is that where you keep your gold?" Patrick pointed at a small iron bound chest secured by a black lock. "Right out of Treasure Island," he said.

"Other treasures," Gert said. "Could you move it over there by those books? Good. Just cover it with the same sheet. Thank you." Patrick made ten trips to the shed, feeling better with each trip. Entering the attic was like going back in time; emerging in the sunlight and walking across the lawn was a return to the present, a promise of future.

"I'll cut the grass before it gets hot," he said.

"Now Patrick, I want you to keep track of your time."

"No need, Gert. I mean—if you wanted me to paint the house or something, that would be different." He liked Gert, but he didn't want to be on call.

"Very well, Patrick. Perhaps you'll take a glass of lemonade." She often seemed amused by him.

"I will," he said.

He took a nap in the afternoon and walked into town refreshed and hungry. The Depresso was mostly empty. He ordered vegetarian chili, cornbread, and a Heineken. "Thanks, Eve." She smiled enigmatically, her mind elsewhere. She, too, was from Michigan, like Sue and Claude, an odd coincidence. Patrick had never been in Michigan, but he imagined deep woods. Eve swayed like a tall pine as she walked.

She was older than Willow. She had three children. Patrick had seen one in her arms and the others swarming up her legs, outside on the patio. She seemed to pace herself—energy for the kids, energy for the customers—somehow remaining beautiful and ready for more. Ready for a different life, maybe. Usually, Patrick couldn't take his eyes from her long strong body, but tonight he saw her more completely, a woman who had to work too hard.

Dylan came out of the kitchen and began to play a low and rolling melody. Patrick felt an equality between them. Dylan played the melody over and over with simple variations, searching for something. Hunting.

In the charged space between Dylan's music and Eve's beauty, Patrick thought about significant digits. Joe Burke was on to something. The rubber met the road at significant digits. Mathematics met reality. Accuracy, significant accuracy, was limited to the precision of the worst measurement involved. It didn't matter that you could calculate an equation to any number of decimal places. The answer couldn't be more accurate than the wobble, the plus or minus, in the coarsest measurement. To not understand this was to think that mathematics was reality. Mathematics was a tool. Physical relationships that were measurable could be expressed in equations, but the equations were models, not reality. You had to keep the distinction in mind or you would think you knew things more precisely than you did.

Dylan disappeared into the kitchen, and Patrick ordered another beer. Models. The word expanded in his mind. Models. Sue was a model. Amber was a model. Equations were models. Mrs. Van Slyke had been a model. Of what? Herself? Hendrik's lover? Women in general? It was really the painting that was the model. Mrs. Van Slyke had modeled for the model. Patrick's mind began to spin.

He continued his line of thought. Mathematics was a tool for making models. So was painting. Science and art had that in common. They made models—of physical reality and of a personal, or human, reality. It was all about model making. Got it! He looked around the room. Got it! No one seemed to notice that he had just figured out a biggie. Probably they all knew it already. He finished his beer and went home, leaving Eve a big tip.

The next morning he thought of Willow as he was closing the front door behind him. Chives were blooming by the shed. He picked a handful of purple blossoms and carried them to Ann's Deli. "Top o' the mornin'," he said to Willow who was behind the counter.

"Oooh," she said. "Chives!" She put them in a small glass with water and set them on the counter. She motioned Patrick to the back of the deli where she put her arms around him.

"Patrick?"

"Mmmm." The hug was warm and intense, but there was work, a sandwich, breakfast . . .

"Good morning," she said happily, letting him go.

"I need a sandwich—got to go to work."

"Roast beef?" She made the sandwich while Patrick chose a pint of orange juice and a banana.

"Want to meet me at the Depresso later?" he asked.

"I can't tonight," she said.

"Oh." He was surprised by his disappointment.

"Tomorrow?" she offered.

"O.K., good. Around five?" That was better. "Oh, Willow . . . " He turned in the doorway. "I've been thinking about science and art again."

"I'll be brave," she promised. Patrick skipped into the News Shop feeling much better. Parker put him on a job on the Wittenberg Road, working with Gino's crew. There was a lot of scraping to be done. Patrick rolled a bandanna the way Wilson did and stripped to the waist.

By break time, he was sweating and relaxed, a large section of one side done. Parker passed out cups of coffee. Patrick ate his banana. Talk jumped from the war to cars to women to growing grass to IBM. There was an IBM plant in Kingston. It had become a symbol of the culture moving in a bad direction. IBM'rs made good money—it was conceded—but they had to wear white shirts and ties; they were considered sell outs, one step removed from robots. Gino told a story about a friend of his who had struggled through a university degree in engineering.

"He was halfway through, dropped out, and got drafted. He also got married, but he couldn't live off base until he was finished with a training program in Alabama. Cleo, his wife, had an apartment in town, and Eddie stayed too late one night. The main gate closed. He had to be in formation, or whatever they

call it, early in the morning before he could get back on base."
Gino sipped coffee. "There was a river along one side of the
base. He walked into it—at night, pitch black, snakes, alligators—
and started swimming. He made it."

Gino shook his head. "After he got out of the Army, he went
back to the university and got a job at IBM. He was O.K. until
one night at Buckman's. Eddie's father is a builder, and some of
his crew were in there. They got on him.

"`Hey Eddie, like that neon tan, Eddie!'

"`Jesus, watch it, he'll hit you with his slide rule.'

"So, Eddie had a few beers, went home, and said, `Neon tan,
Cleo—that's it. Fuck it.' That was the end of IBM for Eddie.
He's doing great now; he's building out in California."

"Right on."

"Pretty good catcher, wasn't he?"

"Damned good." Eddie was one of the saved. Patrick was
beginning to feel that way, too. It was good to be 22 and not
have to keep your mouth shut. Gino got to his feet and stretched.

"What a man!"

"Sit down, Gino."

"No compassion."

"It's lonely at the top," Gino said, trudging toward a ladder.

That evening in the Depresso, Patrick finished the mathematics book. He planned to mail it to Molly on Saturday, when
he usually checked the Post Office for mail. His parents and
Molly were the only people who wrote to him. They were used
to mailing to General Delivery wherever he was living; he hadn't
given them Gert's address. And anyway, summer wasn't going
to last forever; he wasn't sure how long he'd be around Woodstock. Willow. He couldn't really think about her. She was too
new, too big, or something. He felt the sweetness again and was
glad that they were getting together the next night.

Patrick looked out the Depresso window and saw a red Chevy convertible passing with its top down. Willow was riding on the passenger side, her hair blowing. Martin. Willow. So that's why she couldn't meet me, he realized. She looked as though she were having a good time. What do I do now? he wondered.

The next afternoon, Willow was at the Depresso before him, absorbed in a paperback. "Hi, there," Patrick said. She looked up and smiled.

"Hi, Patrick. I brought my largest handkerchief."

"What are you reading?"

"*Balthazar*, by Lawrence Durrell."

"I saw you go by with Martin, yesterday."

"Oh, yeah. Martin took me for a drive and showed me his studio. He has been making recordings."

Patrick looked at her directly and tried to keep his face calm. "Do you like him?"

"I do. He's nice; he asked me a lot of questions."

"He seemed O.K. to me," Patrick admitted.

"Patrick, are you jealous?"

"Umm . . . "

"Tell you what," she said. "Walk me home tonight and I'll show you how much I like him." Patrick started to smile.

"It's a deal." The sun came out from behind a cloud. Willow covered his hand with hers for a moment, and he felt reconnected. "I like you," he said.

"Now don't go overboard, Patrick."

They ate dinner and walked to Byrdcliffe, taking turns pushing Willow's bike. Amber was at Art's; they had the house to themselves. They listened to Dylan and finished a bottle of wine. Patrick undressed for bed with a surprising lack of embarrassment. It seemed natural. They clung to each other and stayed awake late, talking and watching the new moon rise. Willow told him about her parents and her brother and her dissatisfaction with school.

"If you could do anything you wanted, what would you do?" he asked her.

"I think I'd travel and read a lot. Decide what to do and then do it—somewhere. But, do it right, you know?"

"Yeah," Patrick said. "It's the only way."

"Babies, too, some day. Speaking of which—if we're going to keep this up, you better get some of those thingies." Patrick grunted.

"That will be a trip," he said. "Trojans, right? E-Z big tips?"

"They don't care at the drug store," Willow said. "Very big tips."

"Only for you," Patrick said.

"Exactly."

They had to hurry in the morning to get to the Deli in time. Patrick took his sandwich to the News Shop, ate breakfast, and rode to the Wittenberg job with Wilson. When he thought of Willow during the day, he felt easy and excited at the same time. He could actually talk to her. She understood immediately his point that science and art were modeling processes. Better yet, she saw that modeling itself was fundamental—an attempt to understand what was out there and express it with whatever tools you could use. Sleeping with her was so great. Sex. Just the comfort of being next to her. It was such a new experience that he would forget for an hour and then remember with a rush of pleasure.

There was a police car in front of Gert's when Wilson dropped him off after work. "What's happening?" Patrick asked.

"You staying here?"

"Yes."

"Name, please." The cop wrote his name down in a small notebook. "Mrs. Willett's been taken to the hospital," he said.

74

"Oh, no," Patrick said.

"Sick. Heart attack, maybe," the cop said.

"Where is the hospital?"

"Kingston."

"Damn," Patrick said.

"Hope for the best," the cop said, putting his notebook away. "All you can do. She's been around here a long time." Patrick went inside. The house felt empty. There was only one other roomer at the moment, a middle aged guy who kept to himself, a high school teacher from the city. Apparently, he spent a month in Woodstock every summer. Bob. He wasn't around.

Patrick washed and walked into town. He finished a beer quickly and checked the crowd gathering in the Depresso. Claude was at the end of the bar. Patrick approached him. "Hey, Claude."

"Patrick."

"Claude, I've got to go to Kingston."

"Some people have all the luck."

"My landlady got taken to the hospital. Do you know where the hospital is?"

"Benedictine or Kingston?"

"Are there two? I don't know. Kingston, I guess." Claude gave him directions to both. "I don't have a car," Patrick said. Claude looked at him.

"Can you drive?"

"Yes." Claude reached in his pocket and handed Patrick a set of keys.

"It's that '56 Ford pickup out there—the black one with the wood rack."

"Thanks, Claude. What are you going to do?"

"Ahh . . . " Claude glanced around the room and smiled. "We shall see, mon ami. Leave it behind Mower's when you're done, why don't you. Put the keys under the seat. I'll get it in the morning."

"O.K." Patrick left and started up the truck. Three minutes later he was passing the golf course, heading for Kingston on Route 375. Kingston hospital was easy to find, but Gert wasn't there. He drove into the general area where he thought he'd find the Benedictine, trying to remember Claude's directions. He was about to stop and ask when he saw it on a hill. Gert had been admitted.

Patrick explained the situation and was allowed to see her, but only for a minute or two. She was pale and looked fragile. An oxygen tube crossed her face below her nose. Patrick went up close.

"Hi, Gert." She raised her eyebrows in greeting and whispered something he couldn't hear. He bent closer.

"Call Ginger."

Patrick nodded and said, "I will." Ginger was her niece. She lived in St. Louis.

"Patrick."

"Yes?"

"That chest—treasure chest—don't let her see it . . . Mine . . . "

"O.K., Gert, O.K. I'll take care of it. But, you'll be home soon." She smiled faintly and shook her head no.

"My love . . . " she whispered. For a moment she looked young.

"I'll take care of it, Gert." She nodded and closed her eyes. Patrick left, stepping carefully around monitors. He thanked the nurse and went out to the parking lot. It was still light. An ambulance pulled up to an admissions door. It didn't seem right that things outside should be so normal.

He sat unmoving for five minutes and then realized that he was hungry. The Park Diner was on the way out of Kingston, heading towards Woodstock. When Patrick was upset, he ate to settle himself down. He had a steak sandwich, apple pie, and coffee. He was still in shock. How could someone be running around one day and then be totaled the next? Probably she was older than she looked. Damn. There was nothing to do but go home and call her niece.

Climbing the hill to the village green, Patrick had an urge to drive to Willow's, but he decided against it. He had to call Gert's niece, and it wasn't his truck. He parked behind Mower's Market and walked directly home. He found the number in a small book that Gert kept by the phone.

"Ginger?"

"Yes."

"This is Patrick O'Shaunessy calling from Woodstock. I hate to tell you this, but Gert is in the hospital." Ginger said that she would come as soon as possible. She thanked him and hung up. What else could he do?

He left a note for Bob, explaining the situation, and walked back into town. He kept seeing Gert—that clear shake of her head, no. Claude had left the Depresso. Patrick reconsidered driving to Willow's and again decided that he shouldn't. He drank a beer and went home. As he settled into bed, he realized that even though he hadn't seen Willow, she had been there in some sense. He could have seen her. If he had, she would have been helpful. Thinking of that wasn't as good as having her next to him in bed, but it was still good, more than he was used to. "Night, Baby," he said and fell asleep.

Chapter 8

Willow brought home strawberries and made a shortcake. "Real whipped cream," Amber said.

"Of course." Willow reached into the refrigerator. "Trumpet flourish, please."

"Ta da, teedle-oop tee tooo," Amber obliged. "Champagne?"

"A modest vintage, as AhnRee would say. I celebrate. We celebrate."

"You got laid—that's obvious."

Willow poured two glasses. "Biology," she toasted.

"Fucking," Amber said. "Yumm."

"God," Willow said, licking her lips, "strawberries and champagne . . . Truly, it was a revelation."

"It, Patrick?"

"Patrick, yes. The whole thing."

"It wasn't the first time," Amber said.

"It might as well have been." Willow's face lit up.

Amber took another bite of shortcake. "Art's taking me to Nantucket."

"Far out! Moby Dick."

"Shrimp cocktail, gin and tonic—a great way to end the summer. Want to come?"

"End the summer?" Willow blinked. "No. I mean, I'm working. I don't want to end the summer. A terrible idea."

"It is." Amber sipped champagne gravely. "It isn't really the end. Art doesn't want to go until he finishes the outside of his barn. Two weeks, he thinks. But after that, it will be the first or second week in August. We might as well see a few things on the way home—and have a week or so before school."

"School?" Willow twirled her glass. "I'm not going back," she said. "Let this be a formal announcement: I hereby renounce Stanford AND the privileges associated thereunto AND all obligation to write useless papers AND all requirements to be stuck in crowded rooms with people who are dumb, bored, or lying."

"How sweet of you," Amber said.

"Present company excepted, of course."

"I would think long and hard on this one," Amber said. "It's the privileges part. And your family will freak out. What are you going to do?"

Willow put *Highway 61 Revisited* on the stereo. "That's it," she said. "That's the point. I don't know what I'm going to do. But I'm going to find out. I'm going to do what I want and not what someone else wants."

"Is it Patrick? Has he caused you to lose your mind completely?" Amber smiled as she asked, and Willow saw that Amber had already accepted this new reality and was being a good friend, playing devil's advocate.

"It's about finding my mind."

Amber came over and hugged her. "I'll make enough for both of us," she said.

Willow felt a weight lift from her shoulders. She had been thinking about this all day, but it hadn't felt real until she told Amber. It was as though a door opened; a breeze blew around the back of her mind, and the light was brighter. She began to cry. "Hold that door," she said.

"Hold the bottle—is what I'll hold," Amber said, squeezing her. They each knew that they had come to a fork in the road, and that the distance between them would inevitably broaden. They talked late into the night. Amber volunteered to reassure Willow's parents when she returned to California, and Willow promised to write letters from the wild world.

Willow went to bed tired but feeling honest and sure of herself. "It's a new ball game, squirrelie," she said, turning her head toward the woods.

In the morning, she waited anxiously for Patrick in the deli. She rehearsed various greetings, but when he came through the door she took one look and asked him what was the matter.

"Gert is in the hospital."

"Oh no, your nice landlady?" Patrick nodded. "Is it serious?" Patrick raised his arms and let out a breath.

"Yes," he said. "I called her niece in St. Louis. She's coming today, I think. I need a sandwich. Maybe we could meet later?"

"Sure. I'll be at the Depresso. If you don't show up, I'll figure you couldn't make it."

"O.K." He looked relieved. She made him an enormous sandwich and wished that she could hug him, but another customer was waiting. This was the first time she had seen Patrick sad. His expression was calm, resigned, almost delicate. The energy she was accustomed to seeing in his face seemed to have drawn back, turned inward, as though it were trained on maintaining his balance. "I hope I see you later," she said. His answering smile included her in his balance, if that's what it was. She felt more certain than ever that she was moving in the right direction.

On her way home, she stopped to talk with AhnRee who was seated in a director's chair on his lawn. He was sketching an apple tree. "Nice day, huh, AhnRee?"

"Mmm, yes, Willow."

"Pretty." She pointed at the drawing. "I thought you only painted women."

AhnRee looked up from his labor. "One must take a break occasionally. It is good for the eye." He selected another colored pencil and rubbed a few darker patches into the ground beneath the tree. "Tone, Willow."

"Yes, tone." Normally, she would have continued on her way at this point. Hell, normally, she would have waved and not stopped in the first place. AhnRee put down his pencil carefully.

"And are you content here, Willow?" A bit surprising, sometimes, AhnRee.

"I am," she said emphatically. "I love the flowers. It is a wonderful place."

"Pour l'amour." AhnRee smiled. God, this blushing had to stop.

"Right. L'amour," she said. "Patrick," she added.

"Ah, Patrick . . . Is he the one with the red hair?"

"Yes."

"Marvelous," AhnRee said, looking back at the apple tree.

"AhnRee?" He looked back at her. "Amber said that you said I might use your piano some time."

"Of course, Willow, of course. Amber told me that you were musical." He rubbed his stomach. "I am often out in the middle of the day. Just let yourself in."

"Thanks, AhnRee. You are a sweetheart—no matter what they say about you at the Museum of Modern Art."

His face darkened. "Those idiots . . . "

"Just kidding." She skipped away. He was decent, really. She pedaled to the studio, ate a carrot that was getting old, cut up an apple and ate that with a piece of cheddar, and made a mug of tea which she balanced on her stomach as she lay on her bed. She didn't have a violin, and she wasn't sure what she'd

be getting into if she started going over to Tom Merrill's. She
played piano well enough to fool around, to maybe get at what
she was feeling. Her eyes closed, and, without opening them,
she lowered the half empty mug to the stone floor.

An hour later, she brushed her hair and put on a slinky black
T-shirt. She folded a sweater, weighed it down with a book in
the bike basket, and coasted down the mountain. Her favorite
table was empty, a good sign. She ordered a beer and put the
book on the table, but she did not read it, preferring to watch
cars and people pass by, enjoying a feeling of community. I
mean, I live here, she thought. I'm not going back. The words
still thrilled her.

Patrick arrived 45 minutes later looking pretty much as he
had in the morning. "How are ya?" she asked, not wanting to
throw herself at him.

"Thirsty . . . Gert died."

"Damn."

"Yeah. This morning. I just called." She pushed her bottle in his direction and watched him take two long swallows.
"Thanks," he said. "Ginger—that's her niece—is supposed to
arrive tonight. She's staying at the house, so I said I'd be there."

"I'm sorry, Patrick."

"I am, too. I keep seeing Gert lying in that hospital bed all
alone." He paused. "Strange thing happened: she asked me not
to let her niece have a chest that was in the attic. It was like her
last wish. She said the chest was hers. `Mine, my love,' she said.
She was whispering. I could barely hear her. When she said it,
her face changed and she looked like a girl."

"Oh, Patrick."

"She seemed almost happy. I think she was happy."

"Maybe she wasn't so alone," Willow said.

Patrick spread his hands, palms up. "Anyway—I promised,
about the chest."

82

"What are you going to do now?" she asked.

"Thanks, Eve." Patrick took his beer and considered. "Go home, I guess. Wait."

"What about the chest? Is it big?"

"Not very," Patrick said.

"Could you hide it somewhere?"

"I guess I could put it under my bed and pretend that it was mine."

"But, the niece may have seen it before."

"You're right," Patrick said.

"You could put it under the bed with a garbage bag around it—just to hide it. Then we could figure out how to move it later, bring it up to my house or take it to the dump."

"I don't know about the dump," Patrick said. "It would be like throwing her away."

"No dump," Willow said.

"The garbage bag is a good idea. That's what I'll do. So . . . " He stood. "I'll miss you. Love that T-shirt." He meant what was underneath. She wiggled in her chair, pleased.

"I've got the day off tomorrow," she told him. "I'd love to see you."

"Good deal. Here, after work?" They agreed and she watched him leave, walking slowly. She wanted to tell him about her decision, but he had a lot on his mind. It could wait until tomorrow. Also, that would give her another day to make sure it was for real. She knew it was, but it wouldn't hurt to sleep on it one more night.

In the morning, she wrote to the Dean at Stanford, requesting a leave of absence. Willow (Clara) Brown, she signed it. It's my name, damnit, she said to herself. Every one has always called me `Willow.' I can't help it if Dad is a Brahms freak. I mean, there's nothing wrong with Clara, but Willow is my name. She was working herself up to call home. Writing the letter first made the decision more of a fait accompli, even though she hadn't mailed it.

She rode her bike into town and dropped the letter through the slot inside the post office. "That's that," she said and felt better. She called collect from a pay phone and got her mother.

"Hi, Mom."

"Willow, dear!"

"How are you?"

"Just fine. We're all fine. We're worried about you. Are you all right?"

"Never better. Did you get my last letter?"

"The one describing your house and your new friend?"

"Yup. Well—things have moved on. Patrick is more than a friend."

Her mother sighed. "Oh, Willow, I hope you're being careful."

"Mother! Of course. And I've requested a leave of absence from school."

Silence. "I was afraid of this," her mother said. Willow waited. "Your father will have a fit."

"Don't tell him until after he's had his drink."

Silence. Willow braced for where did we go wrong and what's the matter with Stanford. "Baby, are you sure?" The "sure" came from a deep place that resonated with a similar place in Willow.

"Yes," she said instantly. "I'm sure."

"All right, Dear. I'll break it to your father. But you're going to have to deal with him."

"I will. I'll write and let you know my plans. I'm not sure where I'll be this winter. Probably here. I'll let you know."

"Be careful, Dear. I love you."

"I love you, too." Willow put down the phone amazed.

"I mean," she said later to Amber, "I couldn't believe it. She actually talked to me like a grownup, like a woman."

"Far out," Amber said. "I think we better send her some flowers."

"What a good idea!" Willow jumped to her feet and paced the room. "But my father? I can't send flowers to her and not say anything to him. We haven't had it out, yet."

"Your father's pretty cool, considering." Amber meant—for a professor.

"I know," Willow said. "I'll send him the new Dylan album. I'll put a note on it saying, `latest American masterpiece.' Make a joke out of it. He's going to be upset, though."

"He'll get over it. It's not like you're running away with a drug dealer, for God's sake."

"I'll do it this afternoon," Willow said, "before I meet Patrick."

She wrote a short note to go with the album. Her father would be relieved to know that she had requested a leave of absence and would be in good standing at the University. She told him that she needed time to find her own direction. He would think that she was making a mistake, but at least he would hear it from her directly and would recognize that she was serious. She added that there was a guy in town who played piano like Fats Waller. "Love, Willow."

She rode back to the village and ordered flowers for her mother. The Book and Record Shop packaged the Dylan album for her. She slipped in the note and made her second trip of the day to the post office. Not bad, she thought, pedaling to the Depresso. Not bad at all.

"You look cheerful," Patrick said when she arrived.

"It's Pluto," she said, "hanging around Venus again." She bent over and kissed him quickly. "Mercury and Jupiter. You're here early."

"I took the day off."

"So, what happened?" Willow pulled a chair out from the table and sat down.

"Ginger showed up late, around eleven. We talked."

"What's she like?"

"Not bad. Solid. She's married to an accountant—in St. Louis, I told you. She has a couple of kids in college. She is Gert's only close relative. Anyway, she's taking care of things. The house goes to her; she's going to sell it right away. She asked me if I'd take care of the place until then, live for free. I said I would."

"I bet it sells fast," Willow said.

"It should. I guess Gert told her about me, so she trusts me."

"It's a good deal for her," Willow said. "Houses are more attractive when they are lived in, and summer is the perfect time to put it on the market."

Patrick stretched. "I've been thinking," he said.

"About what?"

"About what to do next." He took a drink of beer. "I've been thinking about maybe spending some time on the west coast. Where did you say you were going to school?"

"Woodstock University," she said, laughing. "Oh, Patrick, you are such a sweetie."

"Not," Patrick said.

"I have news, too," Willow said. "I was going to invite you to Deanie's and tell you, but I can't wait."

Patrick sat up straight.

"I quit! I'm not going back. I put in for a leave of absence."

"No shit?"

"Truly."

"Far out." A grin spread slowly across Patrick's face. "What are you going to do?"

"Buy you dinner at Deanie's."

Patrick was surprisingly formal at dinner. He ordered carefully and ate slowly, looking around the restaurant with pleasure. What a sweetie. Willow couldn't get over how comfortable she felt. This was like, life.

"This is my fourth dinner in Deanie's," Patrick said.

"Impressive," she said.

"I always order apple pie," he said.

"Make that two." She told him that she was going to find a way to stay in town. They agreed that it was a good place to be. "I mean, it might be fun here in the winter," she said. "A lot fewer people, I bet."

"Have to get warm coats," Patrick said. They were agreeing, without actually discussing it, to spend the winter together. Patrick walked her all the way home and then walked back after a long hug which stayed with her as she slipped beneath her covers on the porch. How good is this? she asked herself. Very good. As she and Patrick passed through town, a voice had come out of a doorway.

"Patrick, old buddy."

"Hey, Billy," Patrick said, stopping.

"You got a buck for some cigarettes?"

"Yeah, man." Patrick reached into his pocket. "They aren't doing you any good, Billy."

"There's worse."

"I guess . . . This is Willow."

Billy looked her up and down. "Willow, huh—now there's a pretty name. You take care of her, Patrick. She's a good one."

"I'm rotten to the core, Billy," she had said. That started him laughing and coughing.

"You're in trouble, Patrick," he managed to get out.

"I know it," Patrick said. "Well, we'll see you, Billy."

"Obliged. Good night, Willow."

"Good night, Billy."

Tears came to her in bed as she remembered. She and Patrick had walked up the street leaving Billy behind. He had given them his blessing, from a doorway, alone. It was like being married. She felt accepted for the first time as part of a public couple. "Obliged, Billy," she said and slept.

Chapter 9

Fifteen years later, on a November morning, two soccer teams faced each other across a lush green field. San Francisco Bay was distantly visible from the bleachers, blue shading to gray.

"Go, Mustangs!" a dark haired woman in her prime said to a friend joining her. "Hi, Willow."

"Morning, Cree." Willow set down a canvas tote bag and the two exchanged hugs. "Brrrr."

"I know." Cree pointed at the boys who were running together as a whistle blew. "They get to keep warm."

"We do, too. Coffee." Willow pulled a thermos from the bag. "Cocoa. Scones."

"Scones! Willow, you are too much."

"I am the mother of a Mustang," Willow said. "God!"

"We are wild; we conquer," Cree said. "But this team is supposed to be tough. "Go, Bart!" she yelled.

"I'm not supposed to cheer," Willow said. "What do you think? Start with coffee?" She poured two cups. "I couldn't believe it when I saw you at the school."

"It's so weird," Cree said. "It seems like yesterday we were sitting around in Woodstock. And then, in another way, it seems like forever."

"I brought you something." Willow handed a sheet of paper to Cree. "Patrick got in touch with Gino last year, and Gino sent this to him. I copied it for you."

Aesthetic

Muses too are easily bored
and sometimes prefer a tickle
to a grand assault.
You have filled the cathedral with flowers;
organist and choirmaster poised
you stand there expectant
dressed in your best suit.
You may find that
yawning, somnolent with incense,
she has slipped away
around the corner to a restaurant
where a painter
having sketched the
waiter on a paper napkin
uses it to blot the marinara sauce
from his blue silk tie.

Cree read and wrinkled her nose. "That's Gino, all right. I think he's happy in the Maine woods. His relationship is good. He doesn't make any money, but what else is new?" She shook her head. "Well, we got Bart made, anyway."

"Go, Bart!" Willow said. "So, how's your business?"

"Every time I think it's going to die, it surprises me and comes back to life."

"Must be fun going to Italy on buying trips."

"It is fun sometimes. And deductible. How does Patrick like it at the university?"

"He enjoys it," Willow said. "He likes the research best, but he doesn't mind the teaching. The kids love him."

"Of course they do," Cree said. "Now, I'm trying to remember—weren't you into music?"

"I was. I mean, I am. I love it, but I don't perform or anything."

"Bart is pretty good on the piano. I'm thinking of changing to a better teacher."

"I grew up on lessons," Willow said. "I think I had too many. When I was in Woodstock, I used to go up to AhnRee's and play his piano, try to write songs. I found that I couldn't. It was a great disappointment. It was like I was too grooved in the classical; I couldn't get loose, couldn't get away from it. I guess if I were really talented I would have blown it off and done my own thing." She paused. "I wouldn't push it too hard. Nudge, maybe. Scone?"

Cree's face lit up as she bit into the scone. "Mighty fine," she said.

"That's what I do best," Willow said. "It's a wonder I can still see my feet. I'm starting a cafe in January."

"Spectacular! I'll be there. You look terrific. I'm the blimp. I'll think about the music lessons. Thanks, Willow." They watched the Mustangs struggle. The other team was doing most of the attacking. "What's your little one like? . . . Dylan?"

"Right. After Bob," Willow said. "He's more even tempered than Martin, but he's pretty intense. Quiet. He's got a thing for cats, which I take to be a good sign." The attackers lined up for a corner kick. "What ever happened to Joe Burke?"

"Oh, Joe." Cree smiled. "He was something. He and Sally went to Hawaii to live, then they broke up. He's in Maine. They had a daughter. He's remarried, I think."

"He was interesting," Willow said.

"Yeah. If the situation had been a little different . . . " She raised one eyebrow. "I don't think he ever found a place where he fit in. The good old days," Cree said. "When you showed up in Woodstock, you had a friend."

"Amber," Willow said.

"Wasn't she from the Bay Area?"

"Yep—she's in Vancouver, Washington, now. She's a pediatrician. She married a developer with pots of money. They have two spoiled kids."

"She was gorgeous," Cree said.

"She's hanging in there," Willow said. "A line of men was following her around in the mall the last time I saw her."

"Men." Cree shook her head. "They come in handy at a picnic—as my mother used to say. You got the last good one. Patrick is a sweetie."

"As long as you put the pliers back. Jesus." Willow said. There was a great commotion from the attackers as they ran back towards their own goal holding their arms in the air. Mustangs down, one-zip. "Oh, dear."

"We will conquer," Cree said.

"Martin's going to be upset. He's planning to be a World Cup goalie."

"He carries himself like Patrick. Where did the name come from?"

"My father's name is Martin, and also . . . You've got to keep this to yourself." Cree moved closer. "Do you remember Martin Merrill in Woodstock—lived on the Byrdcliffe Road, played banjo and fiddle?"

"Sure," Cree said. "He was around a lot. He had a glamorous mother, right?"

"Right." Willow sipped coffee. "One night, Patrick and I were in the Depresso—about a week before we left town. We'd decided to get married and move to Tallahassee so Patrick could go back to school. We were celebrating. Martin came in, and we told him our plans. He was happy about it and said he had a wedding present for us.

"Patrick said to him, `Wedding present? All right! We don't even have a date.'

"`Soon,' I said.

"`Nobody knows,' Patrick said.

"`My parents already fear the worst," I said.

"`I've got to call my father,' Patrick said.

"Well, when Patrick said that, Martin leaned across the table. `You mean our father, don't you?' I thought Patrick was going to fall off his chair; his mouth opened and nothing came out. `Take it easy,' Martin said. `It's no big deal.'

"`The hell it isn't,' Patrick finally got out.

"`It is and it isn't,' Martin said.

"`How did you know?' Patrick asked.

"`After my dad died—my other dad—I heard my mom talking. She and her best friend were drinking. They thought I was asleep. She'd never said anything. I guess she was worried that the family would throw her out or disown her or something.' Martin looked sad. `You remember things like that. When you showed up, I knew right away.'

"`I thought there was something similar about you two,' I said. Patrick held his hands across the table, extending his fingers.

"`Same hands,' he said. Martin spread his fingers to compare, and then they clasped hands for a moment.

"`I figured you knew,' Martin said, `because of the way you kept watching me.'"

"I'll be damned," Cree said. Willow finished her coffee.

"So, they talked and decided not to rock the boat."

"You never know, do you?" Cree said.

"The next morning, we got up and there was Martin's car in the driveway with a ribbon tied around the hood ornament. He'd come in silently in the middle of the night and left it. There was a note on the seat that said congratulations and that he used Pennzoil in it. The registration was signed over to Patrick. I mean, we didn't even have a car. The next week, away we went, rocking down the coast to a new life."

"Nice, that was nice," Cree said.

"Patrick was fanatic about the car. He changed the oil about once a month. Jesus. It was a great old car though; we used it all through graduate school. It was still running when we came out to the west coast. Patrick's father loved it. We left it with him." There was a second burst of shrill cries; arms held high moved in the other direction. Mustangs even, 1-1.

"See," Cree said. "Are you in touch with Martin?"

"We talk on the phone every once in a while. He still lives in Woodstock; he's got a recording business. We try to visit every couple of years, but you know how it is. Time keeps flying by."

"Scary," Cree said.

"Remember that guy, Wendell? He was a hunk."

"He was."

"Did he ever show up again?"

"Not while I was there," Cree said. "He nearly killed Sam; he had to disappear. He just did get away."

"Was it the FBI or the CIA that Sam was working for?"

"Not sure."

"The bad old, good old days," Willow said.

"Remember Parker?"

"Yeah, Patrick's boss."

"He took off. Left Hildy and the kids for another woman. Sooner or later, just about everyone split up. What's your secret?"

"The dotted line painted down the middle of the house," Willow said. "Patrick needs a visa to enter the kitchen."

The Mustangs were pushed into their end of the field. A fine drizzle began to fall. The two watched, cheeks glowing, as their sons fought back.

"We were talking about Woodstock last night, actually," Willow said. "Patrick's landlady left him a treasure chest when she died. She didn't really leave it to him; she didn't want her family to get it. Patrick says it was her last wish. We've kept it with us ever since. He won't open it."

"Isn't it driving you crazy?"

"I'm dying to know what's in it. He won't open it, though. He says it's ours to respect and to keep private. He says he knows what's in it anyway."

"What?"

"True love."

Cree's eyes went back to the struggle on the field. "Hang on to it, Baby," she said.

Made in the USA
Charleston, SC
28 March 2016